From The Women's Press Ltd
34 Great Sutton Street, London EC1V 0DX

D0129950

Patricia Grace was born in Wellington in 1937, her first collection
of stories, *Waiariki*, was published in 1975 (the first collection of
stories by a Maori woman writer). *Potiki* is her second novel which
was awarded joint third prize of the James Wattie Book of the
Year Awards in New Zealand, 1986. She is the author of two
children's books, *The Kuia and the Spider*, (1981) was the winner of
the 1982 New Zealand Children's Picture Book of the year. She
has taught in primary and secondary schools and in 1985 was the
Writing Fellow at Victoria University in Wellington. She is
married with seven children.

About *Potiki*
'The New Zealand author tells a vivid and mesmerizing story as
she blends tribal myth with political realities and offers shrewd
insights into human nature . . . This unique book is also full of
exotic symbolism . . .' *Publishers Weekly*, U.S.

'I really love the feel of this story. It's the way of telling that is
unique to Patricia Grace. The choice of language is so simple yet so
elegant.' *The New Zealand Listener*

Patricia Grace

Potiki

The Women's Press

First published in Great Britain by
The Women's Press Limited 1987
A member of the Namara Group
34 Great Sutton Street, London EC1V 0DX

Copyright © Patricia Grace 1986
First published by Penguin Books (NZ) Auckland, New Zealand, 1986

British Library Cataloguing in Publication Data

Grace, Patricia
Potiki
I. Title
823 [F]   PR 0639.3.G7

ISBN 0-7043-4081-X

Printed and bound in Great Britain by
Hazell Watson & Viney, Aylesbury, Bucks.

To my Father, in loving memory
Love and thanks to Dick, Keri and Robyn

CONTENTS

PROLOGUE

From the centre,
From the nothing,
Of not seen,
Of not heard,

There comes
A shifting,
A stirring,
And a creeping forward,

There comes
A standing,
A springing,
To an outer circle,

There comes
An intake
Of breath –
Tihe Mauriora.

There was once a carver who spent a lifetime with wood, seeking out and exposing the figures that were hidden there. These eccentric or brave, dour, whimsical, crafty, beguiling, tormenting, tormented or loving figures developed first in the forests, in the tree wombs, but depended on the master with his karakia and his tools, his mind and his heart, his breath and his strangeness to bring them to other birth.

The tree, after a lifetime of fruiting, has, after its first death, a further fruiting at the hands of a master.

This does not mean that the man is master of the tree. Nor is he master of what eventually comes from his hands. He is master only of the skills that bring forward what was already waiting in the womb that is a tree – a tree that may have spent further time as a house or classroom, or a bridge or pier. Or further time could have been spent floating on the sea or river, or sucked into a swamp, or stopping a bank, or sprawled on a beach bleaching among the sand, stones and sun.

It is as though a child brings about the birth of a parent because that which comes from under the master's hand is older than he is, is already ancient.

When the carver dies he leaves behind him a house for the people. He leaves also, part of himself – shavings of heart and being, hunger and anger, love, mischief, hope, desire, elation or despair. He has given the people himself, and he has given the people his ancestors and their own.

And these ancestors come to the people with large heads that may be round or square, pointed or egg-shaped. They have gaping mouths with protruding tongues; but sometimes the tongue is a hand or tail coming through from behind the head, or it is formed into a funnel or divided in two, the two parts pointing in different directions. There will be a reason for the type of head or tongue the figures have been given.

The carved ancestors will be broad-shouldered but short in the trunk and legs, and firm-standing on their three-toed feet. Or their bodies may be long and twisting and scaly, swimmers, shaped for the river or sea.

After the shaping out of the heads, bodies and limbs, the carver begins to smooth the figures and then to enhance them with fine decoration. The final touch is the giving of eyes.

The previous life, the life within the tree womb, was a time of eyelessness, of waiting, swelling, hardening. It was a time of existing, already browed, tongued, shouldered, fingered, sexed, footed, toed, and of waiting to be shown as such. But eyeless. The spinning, dancing eyes are the final gift from the carver, but the eyes are also a gift from the sea.

When all is finished the people have their ancestors. They sleep at their feet, listen to their stories, call them by name, put them in songs and dances, joke with them, become their children, their slaves, their enemies, their friends.

In this way the ancestors are known and remembered. But the carver may not be known or remembered, except by a few. These few, those who grew up with him, or who sat at his elbow, will now and again remember him and will say, 'Yes, yes, I remember him. He worked night and day for the people. He was a master.' They may also add that he was a bit porangi too, or that he was a drunk, a clapmouth, a womaniser, a gambler or a bullshit artist.

Except that he may have been a little porangi, and that he certainly became a master, none of these words would apply to the carver of this chapter of our story. He was a humble and gentle man.

He was the youngest child of middle-aged parents who, because he was sickly as a baby, decided that he should not go to school.

Before the parents died, and when the boy was ten years old, they wrapped him in scarves and put him at the elbow of a master carver who was just at that time beginning the carvings for a new house. This man had no woman. He had no children of his own.

The boy sat and watched and listened and, until he was fourteen, he barely moved except to sweep shavings and smooth and polish wood.

Then one day the master shaped out a new mallet from a piece of rimu and carved a beaky head at the tip of the handle, and gave the head two eyes. He handed the mallet to the boy and said, 'Unwrap yourself from the scarves, son, and begin work. Remember two things,' he said. 'Do not carve anyone in living memory and don't blow on the shavings or your wood will get up and crack you.'

The boy let the scarves fall at his feet, and took the mallet in his hand. At the same time he felt a kicking in his groin.

He never went back into scarves. He dropped them in the place where he had sat at the elbow of his tutor and never went back for them. Later in life he, in turn, became master of his craft. There was no one to match him in his skill, and many would have said also that there were none who could match him as a great storyteller and a teller of histories.

Near the end of his life the man was working on what he knew would be the last house he would ever carve. It was a small and quiet house and he was pleased about that. It had in it the finest work he had ever done.

9

There were no other carvers to help him with his work but the people came every day to cook and care for him, and to paint patterns and weave panels and to help in every possible way. They came especially to listen to his stories which were of living wood, his stories of the ancestors. He told also the histories of patterns and the meanings of patterns to life. He told of the effects of weather and water on wood, and told all the things he had learned at the elbow of his tutor, all the things he had spent a lifetime learning.

At the time when he was about to begin the last poupou for the new house he became ill. With the other poupou, the ones already completed, much discussion, quarrelling and planning had taken place. The people were anxious to have all aspects of their lives and ancestry represented in their new house. They wished to include all the famous ancestors to which they were linked, and also to include the ancestors which linked all people to the earth and the heavens from ancient to future times, and which told people of their relationships to light and growth, and to each other.

But the last poupou had not been discussed, and the people, to give honour to the man, said, 'This one's yours, we'll say nothing. It's for you to decide.'

The man knew that this would be the last piece of work that he would do. He knew that it would take all of his remaining strength and that in fact he would not complete the work at all.

'If I don't finish this one,' he said, 'it is because it cannot yet be finished, and also because I do not have the strength. You must put it in your house finished or not. There is one that I long to do but it cannot yet be completed. There is no one yet who can carry it forward for me because there is a part that is not yet known. There is no one yet who can complete it, that must be done at some future time. When it is known it will be done. And there is something else I must tell you. The part that I do, the figure that I bring out of wood, is from my own living memory. It is forbidden, but it is one that I long to do.' The people did not speak. They could not forbid him. They went away quietly as he turned towards the workshop.

He decided that he would leave himself hollow for this last work, that he would not bring out this final figure with his eyes or his mind, but only with his hands and his heart. And when he spoke to the wood he only said, 'It is the hands and the heart, these hands and this heart that will bring you out of the shadows, these hands and this heart before they go to earth.'

In his old age his eyes were already weak, but he covered the workshop window to darken the room, and his hands and his heart began their work.

The boy at his elbow asked no questions and no one else came near.

After several weeks the carver pulled the cloth from the workshop window. He called the people in and told them that the top figure was done. 'I'll tell you the story,' he said, 'but the lower figure must be left to a future time, for when it is known.

'This is the story of a red-eyed man, who spent his life bent in two, who had no woman and no children of his own. He procreated in wood and gave knowledge out through his elbow. At this elbow of knowledge there is a space which can be left unfilled, always, except for this pattern of scarves. It is like a gap in the memory, a blind piece in the eye, but the pattern of scarves is there.

'His head is wide so that it may contain the histories and sciences of the people, and the chants and patterns, and knowledge concerning the plants and the trees. His forehead is embellished with an intricate pattern to show the status of his knowledge. His eyes are small because of the nearness of his work and because, before my time, he worked in a dim hut with a lantern at night, and worked many hours after dark.

'His tongue is long and fine and swirling, the tongue of a storyteller, and his neck is short so that there is no great distance from his head to his arms. His head and his hands work as one.

'The rounded back and the curve of the chest tell of his stoopiness and his devotion. The arms are short because of the closeness to his work. He has come to us with six fingers

11

on each hand as a sign of the giftedness of his hands.

'The mallet in his right hand rests on his chest, and the mallet is another beating heart.

'His left hand grasps the chisel, and he holds the chisel against his pelvis. The long blade of the chisel becomes his penis thickening to the shape of a man. And this chisel-penis-man resembles himself, like a child generated in wood by the chisel, or by the penis in flesh.

'The eyes of the man and the eyes of the penis-child contain all the colours of the sky and earth and sea, but the child eyes are small, as though not yet fully opened.

'There is no boldening of the legs, and they are not greatly adorned, but they are strong and stand him strongly to his work. And between and below his three-toed feet there is an open place. It is the space for the lower figure, but there is none yet to fill that place. That is for a future time.

'All about the man you can see the representations of his life and work, but with a place at the elbow which will remain always empty except for the pattern of scarves.

'A man can become master of skills in his lifetime but when he dies he may be forgotten, especially if he does not have children of his own. I give him to you so that he will not be forgotten. Let him live in our house.

'"A life for a life" could mean that you give your life to someone who has already given his to you. I was told not to call out anyone in living memory, but it is done. I was told not to give breath to wood but . . . "A life for a life" could mean that you give your life to someone who has already given you his own.'

When the people had gone and he had sent the boy away the carver closed the workshop door. He put his face close to the nostrils of the wood face, and blew.

The next morning the people lifted the poupou from off him and dressed him in fine clothes.

PART ONE

1

Roimata

My name is Roimata Kararaina and I'm married to Hemi Tamihana. We have four children, James, Tangimoana, Manu and Tokowaru-i-te-Marama. We live by the sea, which hems and stitches the scalloped edges of the land. This piece of land is the family land of the Tamihanas. Our houses stand close together on this, the papakainga, and they window the neatened curve of sea. Towards this curve we pitch our eyes constantly, tides of eyes rolling in reverse action to the sea.

The house we live in is the old family home positioned at the centre of the curve. On either side of us are the other Tamihana families and at the far end, near to the hills, is the little wharenui where Hemi's sister Mary goes every day with her brush and polishing cloths to clean and shine. While she works she sings, sometimes softly, sometimes loudly, to herself and to the house.

I have loved Hemi since I was five.

Our son James is like his father – quiet and sure, and with the patience that the earth has. Although first born, it was James who came most easily from between the thighs. His cries caused no earth tremble or sky rumble, no ripple on the midnight hour.

Tangimoana is a year younger than her brother. She is not patient, but is as sharp-edged as the sea rocks, and hears every whisper of the tide. On the night she was born I woke to the pained crying of the sea. We took her name from the sounds that the sea made.

Manu is the youngest that was born to Hemi and me. He is afraid of noise and night, shapes and shadows. He calls and struggles in sleep and we need to wake or comfort him. I knew nothing of his birth. By the time I saw him he was sleeping, a tremor on the mauve closed lids of his eyes.

Tokowaru-i-te-Marama is two years younger than his brother Manu, but he was not born to Hemi and me.

Hemi's sister Mary lives with us too. I have loved her since I was five, since the day we both started school. I knew then that she was someone to love, that she was good and that goodness should have love and care. I looked after her even though she was bigger and older than me.

At school we were given holy pictures and toffees to help us do God's will. God's will was for us to sit still, or stand straight on two feet. It was His will that we pray, that we have clean handkerchiefs, wear aprons, bring pennies for souls, eat our crusts, hold our partner's hand. It was His will that we did not push or dribble, whistle, spit, swear, or make dog's ears in books. But how did you make dog's ears in books? Could there be dog's ears without whole dogs? There could, because there was Little Dog Turpie all taken to pieces and put back together again – perhaps without ears.

It was God's will that we sing the alphabet, the multiplication tables, the hymns and the catechism, and the toffees and the pictures of the suffering saints were kept in a green Jesus tin.

The children who pleased Jesus could put a hand in the green tin for a picture or a toffee – which were little samples of the heaven which was to be the eventual and top reward, where you could reach in and grab a handful and have pictures and toffees poking everywhere between your fingers, and some of them dropping on the ground, or on the clouds that floated past. If you wanted to you could take the whole tin.

We all had slates, and later books and pencils, except for Mary who had a duster and a basket. If she was poked or teased she would sometimes laugh, sometimes cry. If she was unhappy she would come and sit by me.

I listened to the lessons on goodness and knew that Mary was the closest to the Jesus tin, being never calumnious nor detractful, slanderous, murderous, disobedient, covetous, jealous nor deceiving. I knew that she needed my care.

Every morning I would watch Hemi and Mary come into the paddock next to the school on their horse. She would have

16

her ear against Hemi's back and her arms about his waist. Sometimes when they arrived at school she would forget to unlock her arms from round Hemi and he would have to pull her fingers apart. He would see to the horse and I would see to Mary.

She was always excited to be at school, and to see me. 'Roimata, Roimata,' she would say, 'I got suffing in my bag,' and she would smile showing her strange pointy teeth. 'What is it?' I would ask, and she would show me her parcel of sandwiches, her apples or plums, and her clean handkerchief, apron and hand-towel. I would say, 'Good girl,' in Sister Anne's voice, and then take her to put her things away, and to get the cloths and basket from the cupboard for her.

Sometimes Hemi, who was short and wide, would smile at me and tell me that pigtails belonged on pigs' bums. In his shirt next to his heart he carried his spelling book.

Often in the weekends my father would bring me here to this beach, which fronts the Tamihana land. My father would fish, or help the Tamihanas in the gardens, but probably it was the company that was of importance to him. No doubt he had been a lonely man since the death of my mother. I would swim with Mary and her brothers, sister and cousins, or play in the creek or on the hills. Sometimes I would work in the gardens with them, or go to get seafood, or help in the wharekai. Sometimes we would sit on the verandah of this house and talk and sing. I always wished that I could ride on the Tamihanas' horse with my arms round Hemi Tamihana, ear against his back, listening through his back to his heart sounds, but I never did.

Mary stayed at school for three years, dusting the pictures and statues for Sister Anne, or zigzagging about between the desks with her polishing mop. She sang quietly as she dusted and polished, or loudly as she banged the chalk-dusters on the concrete ledge outside. Sometimes she would fall asleep with her head against the statue of Mary, her mouth open a little, showing her strange teeth that looked as though they had been filed.

When Sister Anne left, Mary did not return to school. Hemi left that year too, to attend secondary school. A year later when their father died, Hemi left school altogether to work in the family gardens.

He worked on the land for some years learning all that he could, and intended this to be his life's work, using the knowledge that had been given to him and eventually passing that knowledge on. Then for some years the land had to be left and other work found, but Hemi always knew that he would one day see the land supporting us all again.

As a child I lived with my father in a railway house with a small dark kitchen. The little kitchen window was a window onto curving steel – steel which had come from the earth and was now riveted to it. Our window framed the flying windows, flying eyes, of trains which riveted the senses, carrying them into different mornings, different afternoons and different nights.

But I live now on this other curve that binds the land and sea.

The shore is a place without seed, without nourishment, a scavenged death place. It is the wasteland, too salt for growth, where the sea puts up its dead. Shored seaweed does not take root but dries and piles, its pods splitting in the sun, while bleached land plants crack and turn to bone.

Yet because of being a nothing, a neutral place – not land, not sea – there is freedom on the shore, and rest.

There is freedom to search the nothing, the weed pile, the old wood, the empty shell, the fish skull, searching for the speck, the beginning – or the end that is the beginning.

Hope and desire can rest there, thoughts and feelings can shift with sand grains being sifted by the water and the wind.

I put my bag down there one evening and rested, leaving a way for the nothing, the nothing that can become a pinprick, a stirring. I took warm clothing from my bag and waited through the night for the morning that would become a new beginning.

2

Mary

Mary stood on the step and shook her dusters, then started off over the beach stones to the meeting-house with her bucket of tins and cloths. 'Away, away, away Maria, Away, away, away Maria,' she sang.

She made her way along by the water's edge singing, sometimes talking as she went. Every now and again she would bend and pick something up. If it was something that either lived or could live – a crab, a shellfish or a weed – she threw it into the sea. If it was something that did not live and could not – paper, plastic or tin – she put it in her bucket to take home. 'Now that's better and nice,' she kept saying.

At the far end of the beach she saw a man standing by a small fire dipping tea from a billy. She had not seen him since the summer but she remembered him. 'Joe-billy,' she called. He heard and turned to wave. 'Hey Joe-billy. You come back. Did you?' He called something to her which she did not hear and she went on her way singing to herself, talking, tidying the shore.

As she came nearer to where the wharenui was she left the shoreline and made her way up towards it. Before she went in she called to Granny Tamihana who had been watching out for her, 'You coming Gran?'

'After, darling.'

'Come and see my work.'

'Yes, soon.'

'In my pretty house.'

'Not long.'

'Come and get me.'

'Yes I come and get you after, for our cup of tea.'

'After?'

'Ae, not long.'

Mary stood on the verandah and changed her shoes for slippers and went into the house. 'Here's me,' she said to the house, and put the stone by the door. She opened the window, then put the bucket down and spread the cloths on the floor. She smoothed the cloths, and picking up the can of polish she shook it close to her ear, listening.

She began dusting and polishing the poupou, speaking to the figures and calling each by the name she had given. Sometimes she sang her song to them, 'Away, away, away Maria, Away, away, away Maria.' Sometimes she whispered in their ears.

At twelve o'clock Granny Tamihana hobbled up onto the verandah and called out to her, 'Haere mai te awhina o te iwi. Haere mai ki te kai, haere mai ki te inu ti.'

'See, Gran?'

'Very beautiful my Mary.'

'Beautiful and nice.'

'Very beautiful and nice. . . . You come and have a cup of tea now.'

'Cup of tea.'

'Come and have a cup of tea and a bread.'

'Come back after and do my work.'

'When you had your cup of tea and a kai.'

'Come back after. After,' she said to the house as she followed Granny Tamihana out.

In the kitchen Granny Tamihana's cat whipped itself back and forth along Mary's ankle. It leaned and purred. 'Marama. Well you like me. Do you?'

'Butter you a bread,' Granny Tamihana said. 'And I'll pour us a tea.'

Butter melted on the wedge of bread and the tea steamed. Granny looked at Mary through the steam. 'Put blackberry jam on, dear. Beautiful. Put it on.'

'You like Mary do you? Marama you like Mary?'

'Put jam on. Nice jam.'

Mary stabbed her knife into the jar and levered the jam.

It was lumped with fruit and wine-dark and she spread it into the melting butter.

'Eat it my darling. Drink your tea.'

'Marama you funny tickle cat. You like Mary. Do you?'

'Your butter's dripping, dear.'

Granny Tamihana cut her own slab of bread into little squares. She held each piece between finger and thumb and popped them into her mouth as though she was feeding a bird. She left her tea to cool. Mary bit lumps from her bread which she garbled round in her mouth before swallowing, but she was cautious about the tea.

'Careful of your tea,' Granny Tamihana said.

'Hot,' Mary's elbow jutted. She frowned into her tea.

Afterwards the cat followed her back to the house and curled itself up on the paepae where the sun hit. 'Here's me,' Mary said to the tipuna as she went in. 'Come back to my work now and make you beautiful and nice.'

She moved from one poupou to another with her polish and dusters and a little stool, talking and singing, 'You like my song. Do you?' and she called them by the names she had given them, angry-mother, fighting-man, fish-woman, talking-girl, sad-man, pretty-mother. 'I make you lovely and nice,' she said, 'You like that. Do you? You like Mary. Do you?' She worked her cloth slowly from head to shoulders and down the arms and bodies and legs, standing on her stool to reach the top figure of each post. She worked the cloth carefully into the whakairo, singing, 'Pretty man, pretty mother. You like that? Do you? Mary make you beautiful and nice. Very beautiful and nice.'

Along the right wall near the top end she came to her favourite place. 'Here you are,' she said. 'And here's me.' She stood on her stool, shook the polish can close to her ear then sprayed polish onto the head of the figure and began rubbing the face, and in round the glinting eyes. She worked down over the short neck to the shoulders, and down and along the arms and hands. Then she lay her ear against the chest and listened, not singing or talking, only listening. 'I hear you, loving-man,' she said, then she went on with her work. She rubbed the body lovingly, talking and singing until

21

she came to the penis which had the shape of the figure's stooped, small-eyed self.

It was then that she noticed that one of the penis-man's eyes was missing. 'O poor,' she said, 'O poor. Never matter, never matter, Mary make you better.' She looked about on the floor for the missing eye but could not find it. So she went outside and found a little black stone which she fitted into the socket where the eye had been. She took her cloth and polished the penis and the thighs. When she had finished she stood on the stool again and said, 'There, lovely and nice. You like that. Do you? Loving-man?' And she lay her face against the carved face, and leaned her body against the carved body. Then they put their arms round each other holding each other closely, listening to the beating and the throbbing and the quiet of their hearts. Behind them were the soft whisperings of the sea.

3

Roimata

I decided not to ring or write, but to take what I owned and go there. I needed to go back to the papakainga, and to Hemi and Mary, both of whom I had always loved. Only Hemi could secure me, he being as rooted to the earth as a tree is. Only he could free me from raging forever between earth and sky – which is a predicament of great loneliness and loss.

Looking out of the train, my attention was drawn away from the hills on one side, the sea on the other, the houses holding to the slopes or squatting at the shores. I was drawn away from the groups of people waiting at the stations, their passive faces disguising their ticking lives. I watched instead the seagulls following the boats in, or arcing out over the sea before resting on the grassed playing fields or on the rocks of shore.

Seagulls are the inheritors of the shores where they take up death and renew it, pulling the eyes from fish and pecking the lice that cling to the mouthparts and bone, snatching at the white bloated bodies of porcupine fish which decorate the edge of the water like macabre party balloons, cracking the mussel and pulling it from its shell.

They are also the companions of Tawhiri Matea who dwells forever between Earth and Sky. And sometimes they are his challengers, screaming into the teeth of ice-cold winds, sleet-filled winds, the rolling cloud and thunder. But yet they are free, except from hunger and anger. Free, because although they inhabit the space, they find their place also in and on the sea, and have land as a refuge. The land gives anchorage to the wild matings and also shelters the nest. The gulls, unlike Tawhiri Matea, are not destined to rage in the void forever. They walk the edge, and from the edge fly out, testing and living out their lives.

3

At the last bend was the little railway house that I had left when my father died. There was loneliness there still, and a memory, among other memories, of my father going each morning through the gate in the back fence, stepping up the bank and over the lines to the station with his kai in a little tin box.

The Tamihanas came and stayed with me when he died. They waited with him and me until his family came for him, and then they accompanied us to my father's family place. They told me then what they had always told me, that their homes would always be my homes, and they asked me to return with them. But my father had arranged for me to go away to school. I was fifteen.

I stood on the platform with my bag. It contained all I owned and it wasn't heavy. Then I began the walk that would end where the road ended, a way still familiar although the road had been straightened and sealed by then. It was the way Hemi and Mary had come towards me on their horse each morning, the way my father and I had gone towards them in the weekends needing warmth and company.

I decided that I would not walk along the road but along the beach where I would not be recognised. I was not ready yet for recognition. So I made my way in the edged wind, pulling my feet through the sand. The sea pulled back. The gulls surged ahead of me in strident bands, as though there had been recognition after all. It was as though they expected me, with my load, to rise and cry and follow.

There was only muted light in the sky and the sea receded darkly in shufflings of stone, pulling back between wet rocks. On the road cars went by but I did not turn to watch them.

Before rounding the last corner I sat and rested as night came. The bag was heavy after all, and anyway it would be easier to arrive in the dark – easier to discover, under the shell of night, if there was still a place for me.

When I picked up my bag again the light had gone but I knew the way ahead. I began to cross the barricade of rock that separated one bay from the next.

I had not forgotten how to walk the rock, feeling each step and taking each foothold firmly. The rock was hard and sharp as I traversed it so surely in the dark. And as I stepped down off it at last I knew that the final span of beach ahead would be the most difficult part of my journey.

I looked up and out into the now-dark, to where the hills would be, to where I would see the houses, or lights from houses, set about the shore.

But ahead of me was only the dark. The hills had been obliterated in intense dark. There were no houses, no shadows of houses, no light from houses. There was no sky and no light from sky. Everything, everyone, gone, as though I had come to nowhere and to nothing. At first it seemed like that.

But looking into the distance where I knew the far end of the bay should be, I saw the shadows. I knew then where the people were and why there were no lights on in the houses. There was pale light there at the end of the road, and through the light, people, as shadows passed back and forth.

I knew then that all the people were at the meeting-house, and that in the wharekai the tables would have been set for morning and food prepared. The large pots would be ready in the fireplace, and the wood would have been collected and cut and piled. Inside the meeting-house the beds would have been prepared for the night, and I knew that the recently bereaved would be preparing to lie down for the night beside the recently deceased. I knew all of this in a moment, but didn't know who. I didn't know for whom the genealogies were being recited.

I knew also that I could go no further that night. I would not approach the wharenui at such a late hour, and in any case I did not wish to enter the house of death alone.

The gulls had gone into the dark. In the morning they would pace the light between heavy cloud and sea, a sea that was present at that moment only in its silvered fringe and its strong hearth smell.

I took some warm clothing from my bag and prepared to wait the night through. I am a waiter, a patient watcher of the skies. The tide was beginning to climb the sand, and to drum further out on the reef.

I moved higher up onto the beach, wrapped myself in a blanket and lay down to wait. For part of the night I slept, but most of it I spent awake, seeing only the dark, hearing the insistent nudgings of the sea.

Morning came slowly giving outline to the sea and hills, patterning the squares of houses, moulding the rocks, the power poles and the low scrub. At the far end of the beach around the wharekai, shadows were already moving.

The tide was low again and the birds were shifting, rising, calling, circling under the solid cloud, eyeing the water, dropping, turning, then rising again.

I took a towel from my bag and went down to the sea to wash. The night's cold was still on the water as I waded in. It was a salt cleansing that washed not only the road dust away. It was a discarding, or a renewal, like the washing of hands that takes leave of death and turns one toward the living.

I dressed and spread my towel on the ground to dry. There was more waiting to be done yet so I sat down where I could not be seen, or not recognised. I did not wish to enter the house of death alone so I waited for other visitors that I knew would come.

At mid-morning I heard a bus approaching. It stopped up on the road behind me, and people in it began to stir. I knew that they would have been travelling for most of the night and would now be putting on warm clothing and folding their rugs, and that the women would be tucking greenery in under their headscarves.

The bus started up again and began to move slowly along past the houses to the end of the road where the people would get out, assemble, and wait to be called on to the marae.

I picked up my bag and followed the bus to the assembling place, where I greeted each person and was greeted by each in turn. They put the bag in the bus for me where I would leave it until the formalities were over. The sky had come closer to the earth and white sea was driving onto the shore. I was aware of hunger and glad of the awareness. At the wharenui the people had gathered under the verandah to call us to them.

The first call came and we were treading slowly across the marae. Call and countercall filled the space across the sacred ground, sky shrouded the hills, the sea gashed its forehead on the rocks as the rain began.

At the stomach of the marae we stopped to tangi for death, for the deaths from many ages and the deaths from all the many places, for all the many dead that gathered there with us. We wept for a particular death but I did not yet know whose death, in particular, we wept for. A glance had told me that it was one of Hemi's immediate family that had died as none of them was present on the verandah. They waited for us I knew, inside the house with their deceased.

Then we were called forward again, called in out of the rain. We stepped onto the verandah to remove our shoes, then into the house where we moved to the seating that had been arranged for us. In front of us were the people in dark clothing seated about the finely draped casket. There were the flowers and the photographs.

At one side of the casket were Granny Tamihana and Mary with their heads bowed, and on the other was Mary's older sister Rina, her aunts, and a woman and some children whom I did not know. Adjacent to us where I had not yet looked would be Hemi and his brother Stan with other members of the family.

Absent from among the mourners was Hemi's and Mary's mother, but she was present in the photographs against the wall, and what I knew by then was that she was present amongst us in death.

'Tihei maurimate. . . .'

And twelve years had never been.

'Come forward, come forward. Beach the great canoe of that place. Bring with you the many deceased from there, from that mountain and that river, being the deceased of the many ages of the past and present and the many parts of this land. Many are the dead, as many as the myriads of stars. Assemble the many deceased from there, with the many deceased of the place where we now stand. Assemble them together with the singing bird who sleeps here now, so that they may all be wept for together. . . .'

The paua-shell eyes are many-coloured and vigilant. They encircle the world of day and the world of dreaming, and they encircle the assembled from all places and from all ages. Twelve years had never been.

'Then go on your way, great ones, loved ones, from the many parts of the land. Return to the Homeland, following in the footsteps of those who have gone ahead, following in the footsteps marked out in the beginning. . . .

'And now let there be joining – the dead to the dead, the living to the living. Let the strands fall together. We greet you the living. This hill calls to that mountain, this sea calls to that river, hear the calling. Let the strands fall together entwining so that we are one. . . .'

Behind the eyes the seas drummed, white birds lifted into the storm.

> 'You have gone
> As the song bird
> Flown,
> But my foot is caught
> In the root
> Of the flower tree.
>
> You have gone
> And here I am
> Alone,
> The flowers fall
> Like rain.'

Rain plunged against the roof and wind harried the doorway as one speaker followed another. Bodies moved and eyes glared in the known way, as the legacies of words were spoken and the chants were sung.

'We greet you, ground that we traversed. We greet you house of people, house of people from here . . .

> 'And now
> Lie here sister
> In this ancestral house,
> Listen to the sea sounds
> And the crying of the hills,

28

> Wrap death's fine cloak about you
> And wrap about you also
> Our words and tears,
> Leave us then and go
> Carried by the sounds of waters
> The speakings of words
> Go to the night everlasting
> Where the many gather . . .

'And living family we hear your call. We greet you and divide sorrow amongst all of us so that it may be lessened.

> 'We are split and empty
> As the shell of the kihikihi
> Which clings to the bole of a tree
> But hear the cry
> Tatarakihi tatarakihi.
> We give you our greetings. Greetings to all of us.'

We stood and moved to greet the people, to hongi, to embrace, to tangi for this particular loss and for the fact of death. I moved gradually to greet and to tangi with old Granny Tamihana who had stood to carry out the arduous task of sorrowing, and then I moved to Mary who had not forgotten me. We pressed our noses, we kissed and embraced. 'Look at Mummy. She's so pretty. She's so nice. Is she, Roimata?'

I looked into the casket at the thin quiet face and dark hair. They had dressed her in a blouse of white chenille and lace, and pinned to it was a Mary of Sorrows medallion that I remembered she always wore. But that seemed so long ago. At her throat was a locket that she wore on special occasions, open now, and showing the tiny photographs of the son and daughter who had died as children. Covering her to the waist was the finely woven cloak with its feather border, and on top of that the mere pounamu. 'Pretty,' I said. Twelve years, but I had not forgotten how to talk to Mary. 'Pretty, and nice.'

The Sister and the aunts held me to them and we wept for all sorrow that had occurred since last we had met, but especially for this one. Then I greeted the woman and children that I did not know – but knowing that the woman could have been Hemi's wife, and that the children could be his. Hemi and I greeted each other formally, then held each other closely as we wept for the death of his mother, and for all death. Then I moved to greet his brother and cousins in a similar way.

As we went out to wash there was another group assembling at the edge of the marae.

I did not speak to Hemi again until the evening of the day his mother was buried, or at least I did not speak at length to him. It had been a busy time as I set about to help with catering and caring for the many people who came. We set and cleared the long tables and cleaned and refilled the big pots many times a day. Each evening after karakia we worked well into the night baking bread and preparing meat and vegetables for the next day. It was as though twelve years had never been as I fitted myself back into the known routines.

Hemi stayed mainly in the wharenui where arrangements for his mother were discussed and where decisions were made. He was there to greet and to be greeted by each group and each individual that came.

That night after the work had been done and many of the visitors had gone he sat by me and said, 'When did you hear?' He prompted nothing further from me.

'I didn't hear,' I said, 'I didn't know. . . .'

'So that wasn't the reason.'

'Just off the plane . . . the previous day. Walked from the station, and when I got to the corner I knew it was . . . someone.'

'So . . . on your own. Not with that bus, that group. I wondered. . . .'

'Joined them at the gate, next morning.'

'You were coming but it wasn't because of her.'

'It was night when I got here, it was dark. I saw the lights on . . . down the end here. It was too late . . . so I waited.'

'All night.'

'I knew it was . . . someone, but I didn't know who. When

I got into the house, saw the family, the photos, that was when. . . .'

'But it wasn't for that. You were coming.' It wasn't a question.

People were singing – songs for the living, as the concerns of death moved to the outer edges of the spiral. Rina and Joyce pulled us up to join in the action songs, which I found I had not forgotten:

> 'Titiro ki a Rona
> Ki runga i te rangi
> Mo te riri
> O te marama e,
>
> Titiro ki te rakau
> Mau i te ringaringa
> Ki runga
> I te rangi e. . . .'

It was as I had thought. One became a sky dweller by accident, or by way of punishment, not on purpose. Rona was a lonely figure up there in her moon-house, holding on to her little tree and her calabashes. Had she grasped a more sturdy tree, a more heavily rooted tree, she could perhaps have stood against the anger of the moon. Joyce was Hemi's brother's wife and the children that I hadn't known were their children.

'So you came,' he said, but still it was not a question.

'I felt as though I was floating,' I said, 'As though there was nothing . . . important.'

'And you came.' We did not speak for a long time after that. We joined in the singing and the talk going on about us. Then Hemi said, 'I didn't think there would be anyone. . . .'

'I need at least a toehold. . . .'

'Anyone . . . for me.'

'Somewhere.'

'Everything's meant,' he said, 'I've always believed it. And . . . I'm happy.'

4

Roimata

The sea was grey and calm after a week of wind and bowling waves. There was a humid quiet and a flat grey sky.

When James and Tangimoana arrived home from school I always put the jug on to boil. We made hot drinks and waited for Mary to come home. When Mary heard the school bus arrive she would fold her cloths and put them into her bucket with the polish. She would shut the window and the door of the house then come home so that we could all have a cup of tea together. Sometimes she would bring Granny's cat with her.

That morning I had worried about Mary because she'd complained of pain, but I had not been able to persuade her to stay home and rest. And that afternoon she had forgotten to come. It is easy for her to forget. By then we should have heard her open the gate, heard her singing or talking as she came round the side of the house, and heard her putting her bucket and cloths away and taking her shoes off in the porch.

When she didn't arrive I went to the front window to watch out for her, and saw her walking awkwardly down onto the beach by the meeting-house. She has her own way of walking, moving her short wide body from side to side, but that day she walked differently, more awkwardly – and yet there was something familiar. . . . She did not have her bucket with her but I knew it was easy for her to forget. I saw her sit down, going out of sight behind where the beach stones had piled.

We drank our tea while we waited for her. I kept going to the window and after a while I saw her stand and walk right to the edge of the water holding something. I wondered what the week's rough seas had left on the shore to interest her. Mary is a tidier. She will clear debris from the beach,

32

either bringing what she has found home in her bucket, or returning it to the sea.

'Tangimoana,' I said, 'Run down to the beach and bring Aunty Mary home.' I expected Tangi to complain but she had been watching too. Curiosity always moves her. She was six years old, small and thin, and had a mean mouth.

'She's a maddie,' she said, 'A maddie-porangi. Aunty Mary's such a maddie-porangi.'

'You stop that Tangimoana. Don't you . . .' but she had gone. Her red tee-shirt was a flag of colour against the grey sea, grey stones, grey sky.

I watched Tangimoana as she stood and called to Mary from the top of the beach, but Mary didn't stop or turn. She walked into the water still holding whatever it was, close to her face, as though she could be eating or licking it. I knew then that I should not have sent Tangimoana to get Mary but should have gone to get her myself.

Tangimoana stood at the top of the beach stamping her feet and I knew she was shouting at Mary. I saw her go down and follow Mary into the water. Then I saw her thump Mary with her little fist, and pull and snatch at whatever it was that Mary held in her arms.

Then Tangimoana began to hurry home – running, walking, running, and Mary was still standing to her waist in the sea, looking back.

I hurried out to meet Tangimoana calling, 'You're naughty, you're mean Tangimoana. Why didn't you bring her, why didn't you wait, what were you screeching about?'

And Tangi called out, 'Mum, Mum, it's something! She was putting it in the water. O Mummy it isn't a fish!'

Tangi never cries from anything except temper but I could see she was close to crying.

What she held out to me, what I took from her, was a misshapen and cauled baby boy.

I peeled the piece of skin from the little face and there were such small sounds coming from the stretching mouth. The skin was the colour of stone. My hands moved themselves to turn the boy upside down and I shook him lightly so that he began to cry. Then I hurried inside and took a warm towel from the hot-water cupboard to wrap him in.

'She was going to chuck it away. Mum, Mum, in the sea!'

'Where was it. . . ? Where did she. . . ?'

But Tangimoana was a breath ahead of me.

'Mummy, Mummy, I think she borned it.'

I remembered Mary's clumsiness as she had walked from the top of the beach, more awkward than her usual awkward manner, and I knew that what Tangimoana had just said was true.

'She's a porangi. O I told you, I said. . . .'

'Stop that, Tangi. Stop it! You have to help me. You have to get Mary. . . .'

'Uncle Stan's gone. He was coming out his gate.'

'Tangi, what else. . . ? Was there anything. . . ?'

'She bit it with her wicked teeth. . . .'

'Tangi you behave. . . !'

'And it slid and dropped right into the sea.'

'Run fast Tangimoana, and tell Uncle Stan to bring Mary and Granny. Tell him to bring them in his car, straight away. Now!'

James came in followed by Manu. He stopped in fright by the door – not, I believe, because of the wrapped snuffling bundle that I held, but because of the shock that he saw on my face.

'A baby,' I said, 'A baby boy. Tangimoana took him . . . from Aunty Mary and brought him home.'

I was listening for Stan's car and wondering and worrying about Mary. At the same time I was feeling appalled at the humpy shape of the child's back and the turned wispiness of his legs.

'James, go and open the door and the gate,' I said as I heard the car coming. I spread a rug on the settee and put the baby down.

Granny Tamihana and Stan held a blanket about Mary as they brought her in.

'Don't know what she was doing in the sea,' Stan said, 'And she's not herself. Nothing to say. And . . . there's blood.'

'Our Mary a little bit sick,' said Granny.

'Don't ask her anything, not yet.' I showed them the baby.

'She had it, just now. . . .'

'Had?'

'Gave birth to, down on the beach.'

They looked in some disbelief at the bundle that I held out to them.

'It must be hers,' I said.

'Well someone done wrong to her,' said Granny. 'Come on, darling, you never mind. Someone done wrong to you. Come on Granny put you to bed.'

It was such a sad thing to see Mary so quiet and so expressionless.

'I'll help you get her into bed Gran, and you see how she is.'

'Has the rest come?'

'It dropped . . . into the sea. Tangimoana said. . . .'

'I'll go and get it,' said Stan.

'Bring it so we can do right, bury it right,' Granny Tamihana said.

'I reckon it was that old scrounger,' said Stan as he went out, 'Always hanging round here. Well we'll see about that. . . .'

'Tangi you bring Gran the towels from the cupboard, and James you make a warm milk drink for Mary, please Son.' Manu was lying by the now-sleeping baby, gently touching the baby's long, damp black hair.

It was Mary who had first given the old man the name of Joe-billy. He came every summer with his billy and his bundle to camp for a month or two on the beach. He kept to himself for the most part but he had become a friend to the children and to Mary. They were always excited to wake, and looking out, to see the smoke from his fire and know that he had come. James and Tangimoana had sometimes spent evenings with him fishing from the beach. He would dip tea for them out of the billy and toast slices of bread. He had always seemed a kind man. It was difficult to believe that he would lie with Mary knowing that she really was a child still, and that she would never come to an understanding of it all. I was angry and shaken as I helped Granny Tamihana to attend to her.

35

And Mary was wordless and unmoving as we washed her, then helped her to drink the warm milk that James had brought.

When we had finished with Mary and made her comfortable Granny Tamihana bathed the baby's head and blew sharply onto his temples. She blew his mouth and nostrils, and with two fingers lightly massaged his chest until the mucus began to drain freely. She took a pendant from her ear and put it on the blanket beside him. 'Tokowaru-i-te-Marama. Ko Tokowaru-i-te-Marama te ingoa o tenei,' she said.

When she had finished Manu took up his place beside the baby again, and went to sleep.

5

Roimata

When Manu turned five I went with him every day for two weeks and left him in the porch of the school with Tangi-moana and James each holding a hand. By ten o'clock he would be running back home along the beach calling to me and to Mary, and to his little brother. He would be trembling and exhausted, and at night he would call out and cry in his sleep. If I asked him why he cried, why he ran away from school, he would say there were cracks in the floor, and begin to cry again.

'He's frightened,' I said to Hemi, 'and he's exhausted and pale.'

'Keep him home,' Hemi said.

'He says there are cracks in the floor, and the kids fizz like bees. He thinks he'll disappear.'

'He'd be better here with you. We don't want to . . . lose him.'

'He says they've got no stories for him. . . .'

'School's all right for some, but you don't always find what's right for you,' Hemi said.

'He's scared. And he misses his little brother so much. They've never been separated since Toko was born, and it doesn't seem right. . . .'

'He's better here with you. Let him stay home. Everything we need is here, and they learn all right with us. Better for Toko too, when the time comes.' Hemi has a way of seeing clearly the things that matter most.

So I kept Manu home with me, and Toko, when he was five, decided to stay home too. Despite his physical disabilities and his periods in hospital, Toko could have gone to school if he had wanted to. His learning is so quick and sure, and

37

he is too watchful to allow himself to slip and disappear. All
stories belong to him.

At first when I thought about keeping Manu home I planned
that our porch would become a classroom, a miniature of
other classrooms I had taught in. I thought of desks and books,
blackboards, chalk-dust, and coloured pictures of gardens,
beaches and streets. There would be a table, I thought, where
we would have potato hedgehogs and wheat people – mother,
father and child – with their green growing hair to be
measured and cut. There would be eggs and feathers and
favourite stones, and beans sprouting in a tray of wet cotton.
There would be multiplication tables and number lines,
jigsaws, scissors and paint, and an alphabet frieze, and clocks
that told us when to start and stop.

But then I remembered what we had talked about, that
schools were all right for some, but that you didn't always
find what was right. I thought of Manu saying that there were
no stories for him, and that there were cracks in the floor
and kids that fizzed like bees. I remembered that everything
we needed was here.

What would be right then for a little one who called out
in sleep, and whose eyes let too much in? What would be
right for one who didn't belong in schools, or rather to whom
schools did not belong? What was right for one who had a
fear of disappearing and who could not find his stories?

Then I knew that nothing need be different. 'Everything
we need is here. We learn what we need and want to learn,
and all of it is here,' I said to Hemi, but he had always known
it. We needed just to live our lives, seek out our stories and
share them with each other.

So I didn't become the teacher, or rather didn't become
once more the teacher that I had trained to be. There was
no need for a room to be changed because a boy had become
five and could not find himself in schools. I became instead
a teller of stories, a listener to stories, a writer and a reader
of stories, an enactor, a collector and a maker of stories. But
I only shared in this. What really happened was that we all

became all of these things – tellers, listeners, readers, writers, teachers and learners together.

The stories that I had to share were childhood stories of the railway house, of school and holy pictures, and a boy and a girl on a horse. They were of games and gardens, and loneliness, and of looking out at trains. They were of going away and returning, and of death and birth.

I had other stories too, known stories from before life and death and remembering, from before the time of the woman lonely in the moon. Given stories. But 'before life and death and remembering' is only what I had always thought. It was a new discovery to find that these stories were, after all, about our own lives, were not distant, that there was no past or future, that all time is a now-time, centred in the being. It was a new realisation that the centred being in this now-time simply reaches out in any direction towards the outer circles, these outer circles being named 'past' and 'future' only for our convenience. The being reaches out to grasp those adornments that become part of the self. So the 'now' is a giving and a receiving between the inner and the outer reaches, but the enormous difficulty is to achieve refinement in reciprocity, because the wheel, the spiral, is balanced so exquisitely. These are the things I came to realise as we told and retold our own-centre stories.

When James and Tangimoana came home from school they brought their stories with them. School had a place for them. They had no fear of disappearing into cracks in the floors, the one being too careful and sure, the other too sharp and nimblefooted.

James's school stories were about the earth and the universe. This school earth was divided by lines – latitude, longitude and equator. The people of this school earth lived in countries which were in continents, oceans and hemispheres. Some of the people in some of the school countries lived in eggshells on paper snow, some lived in matchstick villages by a paint sea crowded with dot-eyed fish. Others sat by cellophane fires with silver chocolate-wrap feathers in their hair, and others had cardboard homes behind a paper wall that could not be climbed by the sea.

It was the charted rainfall, the sun, the hurricanes, the monsoons, the typhoons and snow, and it was the cross sections of mountains, rivers, land and soil that told people what their lives would be.

This school earth was an orange – tilted, and squeezed top and bottom – which took a whole day to turn, and a whole year to circumnavigate the tennis-ball sun. And it slotted into a universe which could be viewed through a peep-hole in a cardboard box, paper planets dangling from threads against navy-blue space, and light coming in through the cellophaned cutout in the box's lid.

James had stories also of light and sound, of multiplying, dividing, adding and taking away. And we found that we all had stories of all these things, and that one dovetailed into another.

Tangimoana had stories of people. Some of these were book stories of queens and kings, monsters, charmers, murderers, ghosts, orphans, demons and saints. And we had our own heroes and heroines, enchanters, wrongdoers, outcasts and magians to add to these stories from books.

Some of her stories were living stories of the people about her – raw-handed, mad Margaret at school who stared and pointed into the corners of the room, Billy who cried, Sila dressed in gowns and flowers, Julieann who made pencils and rubbers disappear by touch. Some of the stories were about herself, and about us too. She wrote all of her stories down in old exercise books or on scraps of paper. They were stories, poems, lines, pages, which she left for us to find and read.

In the evenings Hemi would come home with his work stories, which were stories of men with swinging knives and blood on their hands, who pulled the hides from the hanging carcasses, then cut and sliced, and sent the carcasses swinging down the chains. Their days were enfolded in the smell of offal burning, and everyone dressed as white as doctors. He told of when he was a boy and of how he had been given work and knowledge on behalf of people.

Mary would tell us her stories too, which were not always

40

exactly the same if you listened carefully, of talking-man and angry-wife, trick-man and singing-girl, pretty-man and fighting-mother and no one for the loving-man with the big big hammer.

There were the stories that Granny Tamihana had to tell which were weavings of sorrow and joy, of land and tides, sickness, death, hunger and work. There were stories that other members of the whanau told as they came to share our mornings with us.

Then there were the stories from newspapers and television that we read and viewed each day. And there were the stories we found in library books which we went to exchange every few weeks.

Gradually the stories were built upon, or they changed. None changed more than Hemi's which told more and more about people who were not working any more because there was no work for them, and of people who were beginning to be cold and poor. More and more he was telling about the land and how the land and the sea could care for us. It could care for those who had gone away too, but who would return now that work was hard to find. 'There are things I can tell you in stories,' he said, 'But I can show you too, and then you'll really know that everything we need is here.'

And so it was because of our little bird that stories became, once more, an important part of all our lives, the lives of all the whanau. And although the stories all had different voices, and came from different times and places and understandings, though some were shown, enacted or written rather than told, each one was like a puzzle piece which tongued or grooved neatly to another. And this train of stories defined our lives, curving out from points on the spiral in ever-widening circles from which neither beginnings nor endings could be defined.

6

Toko

I know the story of my birth. When I was born my borning mother was not much older than me, and now I am older than she is.

I don't know who my making father is. Roimata says that my making father could have been an old man with a rolled blanket and a tin can that used to visit here once. Well never mind. My making father could be a ghost, or a tree, or a tin-can man, but it does not matter. I have Hemi who is father to me.

I was born on the beach stones on a day with no colour and my borning mother carried me into the water. She would have left me there for the birds, mistaking me for something she had found. Or she could have kept walking with me out into the water until the sea closed over us, and we would both have belonged to the fishes. But my sister Tangimoana, in her red shirt, came and snatched me away from my first drowning and hurried home with me.

Then Roimata, who is a mother to me, took me and peeled the skin from my two-colour eyes so that I could see. She turned me up to let the stone fall from my throat, then she shook breath into me and wrapped me in warm towels. My brother lay down by me and slept.

Soon my Granny Tamihana came with all her gifts. She blew all wrong things away to clear and free me, and rubbed the bubbles up to save me from my second drowning. She gave me magic from by her ear, and gave a name from when she was a girl.

My Uncle Stan went down to the sea to look for my other skin but the water held too much grey. He dived and searched until dark, and my father Hemi when he came home, and my brother James and all the people helped too. They searched but they could not find my old shell to bring home and bury. My old self went to the stomach of a fish, and for a long time after that there could be no fishing by anyone, no shellfishing, no swimming, no playing in the sea.

Perhaps it is the magic from Granny's ear that gives me my special knowing, and which makes up for my crooked-ness and my almost drowning. But I have been given other gifts from before I was born. I know all of my stories. There was nothing anyone could do about the crookedness of me.

7

Roimata

My children and their cousins were like cicadas, kihikihi, chittering in the sun. They would pile the beach wood at one end of the strip of sand, keeping aside the long, straight pieces which would be used as weapons.

We had become tellers, listeners, readers, writers, enactors and collectors of stories. And games are stories too, not just swallowers of time, or buds without fruit. Games, as played-out stories, also define our lives – but I did not understand the children's war games. I could not tell what their war games were a reflection of.

When we were children we had played our war games too. The beach had been a place of battle for different kinds of wars. In one war the beach was a battlefield lined with soldiers, and beach stones were hand grenades lobbed into driftwood tanks, or torpedoes screaming towards submarine targets. Beach sticks were rifles with bayonets tied to their barrels. Aeroplane arms ran the sand amid shell and machine-gun fire. Every death was heroic and dramatic, but done with quickly – every hero dying and regaining life again and again.

The beach was a far-away country where we played out what had come to us through newspaper, radio and film. Because then, somewhere across the sea, there was a real war that gave recognition to our games.

And there were other wars from across the sea too, but which had come from other times. On Saturdays we went to the pictures, on Sundays we made the stories our own. The beach became rock and desert and lawless towns. We rode driftwood horses and had wood six-shooters, arrows and bows. Or sometimes we stood on log ships driving the enemy into the sea with white swords.

In yet other war games we fortified our villages and fought

44

with clubs and taiaha in battles which mirrored, not the battles shot into our lives from other countries, but the running, leaping, dancing battles which came to our lives in our own stories from a different age.

But I could not grasp the meaning of the war games that the kihikihi played. Their games did not seem to be of a past, or of another country. There were no guns, no vehicles of war, no clubs or swords. The sticks were sticks, the stones were stones, the big logs were barricades, no more than that. There were no new voices and no new names. There was nothing different in clothing except for light bands round their foreheads which they sometimes wore. There was no enemy, or rather the enemy was not known.

So all that could be understood and remembered was that Tumatauenga withstood all challenge in the beginning, and that he has stood astride the earth since and will forever. There was no comfort in remembering it.

There was no comfort in remembering that Tu became stronger, not weaker with challenge. The onslaught by Tawhiri caused Tu to place his feet even more firmly on the earth. Tawhiri thus strengthened Tu, as conflict always strengthens conflict.

Not even Tane and Tangaroa could stand against their brother when he took revenge against those who had not assisted him. They could only stand by as Tu pounded the heads of their children and cooked and swallowed them. There could have been only one comfort for Tane and Tangaroa in all of this, and that was in knowing that death becomes life – that what goes down under the club of Tu and enters Tu's belly becomes new life in the body of the earth. Death is a seeding.

But there was no comfort for me in remembering these things as I turned the ancient stories in my mind.

The children would move forward, running towards the walls of piled wood. They would hurl the stones, then run in yelling waves, up and over the barricades hitting and jabbing with the long sticks before turning and retreating. There was no enemy – or the enemy was unknown and unseen, behind the barricade.

There was nothing there that came from film or ancient story. There were no gunfighters or marching armies, or cut-throats, no battlefields or fortified villages, or quiet deadly pathways through a jungle.

'What are the wars about, Toko?' I asked.

'Fighting,' he said.

'But fighting who?'

'Just enemies.'

'And who are they? Who is the enemy?'

'We don't know yet, but they have stolen from us.'

'What have they stolen?'

'We don't know yet but it's something to do with our lives.'

'And where? What place, what country?'

'No place, or just wherever you are, because it's not good to have your life taken out.'

'Well what is it then, the life that's being stolen?'

'We don't know yet, but it might be something like a glowing heart of all special colours, pink, green, brown, blue, purple and silver.'

'And where? Is it on the moon, or out in space, in the desert, out at sea?'

'It's just an ordinary place. It's where you are.'

'And what will happen?'

'We don't know. We don't know if we will get our purple, pink and silver back that has been snatched from our throats and our eyes. We don't want our special glowing colours pulled from the insides of us and dropped on the road under the feet that sound like hammers.'

'Whose feet, tramping on the red and silver?'

'We don't know, we can't see them, but I think one day we'll know.'

Toko is a gift that we have been given, and he has gifts. He has a special knowing. I held him to me and felt afraid.

'Do you know about the kihikihi?' I asked him.

'Yes,' he said. 'They are already old when they are born. They leave their old lives clinging to a tree and in their new lives they are given glass wings. Their eyes are blood-red jewels. They fly up to drum in the sun and birds drop down from the sky.'

46

8

Toko

I know the story of when I was five. The story has been told to me by my mother Roimata, my father Hemi, my sister Tangimoana, and my brothers James and Manu. But also it is a remembered story. Five is old enough to remember from, and five is not very long ago.

It is a big fish story.

Hemi needed bait for the next day's fishing, and after tea he asked James and Tangimoana to go out on the lagoon with him to catch herrings. James went to the shed to get the little herring lines with their tiny silver hooks. My father cut up little pieces of bacon fat for bait.

I followed James to the shed, climbed up and took a heavy line from the shelf.

'We don't need that one,' James said.

'I need it,' I said.

James didn't argue with me. He never minded and always let me do whatever I wanted to do. I followed him back to the house taking the big line with me.

'That's no good, we don't need that,' Tangimoana said.

'I need it for my big fish,' I told her. She did mind.

'Not in the lagoon. There aren't any big fish in the lagoon, only little ones.'

'There is. There's a big fish for me,' I said.

'Only herrings, and anyway you can't come.'

But I knew there was a big fish for me, and I knew that I would go. That's what I remember very clearly about that night. I remember the sureness that I had. I remember clearly that I *knew*. I knew that I would go. I knew that there would be a big fish for me.

My father Hemi said, 'You can come Boyboy if you sit still in the boat. I'll give you a little line but you be careful.'

'I got my line,' I said, 'For my big fish.'

Hemi did not argue with me, but my sister Tangi stared at my face, and I think she was angry with me. Well I don't really remember Tangimoana staring at my face, but I know that's what she always does. She stares at your face. No one can escape from her.

The day was just changing to be night, and the sea was like chocolate wrapping that you've smoothed with the nail of your thumb. I did not feel small that night the way the sea can make you feel small sometimes. I carried my big line with me. My mother Roimata had taken one of the hooks off to make it safer, but it didn't matter because it was only one big fish that I was going to catch. I only wanted one big hook for my one big fish. She put a piece of paua on my one big hook. The piece of paua was for bait, but it was also to cover the barb so that it would not hook itself into me. I do not remember that, but I've been told.

Tangi and James carried an oar each and I carried only my line, but I did not feel small. I didn't feel small when Tangimoana and James helped Hemi pull the dinghy down to the water. I hurried in my special boots and Hemi lifted me into the bow.

Two pulls and we were out into the middle of the lagoon. Tangi put bread on to the water to bring the herrings. The water was a soft orange colour I remember, and little herrings put their mouths to the water's skin making sharp circles which widened and widened on the surface of the water.

My father and my brother and sister pulled the lines about over the surface of the water and the herrings popped onto them time after time. They wanted me to have a little line so that I could catch herrings too. They were all enjoying themselves I remember – and I've been told – but I did not want to have enjoyment and herrings. I knew why I waited. I was quiet and excited, and I knew. There was a big tin in the dinghy and it was quickly getting filled with herrings.

Soon the light went off the water and then the sea was only a sound – a soft sucking sound and a fish splash sound. When the dark came so did the cold, and I've been told Hemi put a jersey on me. I do not remember the cold but I know it is true that Hemi would have taken a jersey for me, and that he would have put it on me when the sun went down. After dark the sky was white with stars. Tangimoana has told me that. I don't remember the sky of stars, or the whiteness of the stars, my thoughts were in the water. The sky was like a sea full of herrings Tangimoana has told me, but I have no memory of that. My thoughts were not in the sky.

James wanted me to have his line for a little while because he cannot enjoy without sharing. But I waited strongly holding my strong line with its big old hook that had been fixed for deep water, and its heavy sinker bigger than my fist. I don't remember the stars or the cold, or my brother James wanting to share his line with me, or the sinker bigger than my fist, though I've been told. But I remember waiting, and the light going, and the soft splash sounds of the water with all the colour gone.

I remember when the pull came. James, who was sitting by me, grabbed and held onto me so that I wouldn't go over the side. I held on hard to my line. I remember that for a moment there was nothing else, only holding – me holding the line, James holding me. Hemi took the other end of my line, unrolled some of it and tied it to the seat.

'Hold him, Son,' he said to James. Then he said to me, 'Let go now, Boyboy. It's tied.'

I didn't hear him, and I don't remember. I was holding and pulling, and James was holding me. 'My fish, my big fish,' I remember calling.

And then I remember my father Hemi taking my hands and saying, 'Hold it lightly now, Boyboy. The line is tied.' He made me look to where he had tied the line to the seat. 'You'll cut your hands,' he said, 'if you hold the line too tightly.' He stopped me from pulling. 'You'll have us all in the sea. Stop pulling now, let go now and we'll row your big fish into shore.'

I remember that Tangimoana was calling out to my mother Roimata and my mother Mary and my brother Manu and some others who had gathered, and who were sitting on the beach round a little fire they had lit there. 'He got it,' she called. 'Boyboy got it. Toko caught his big fish.'

'Stay there with your line,' Hemi told me when he ran the dinghy up on to the beach. He and Tangi and James got out. My uncles and my cousins helped them to get the dinghy with me in it, onto dry shore. Hemi lifted me out and we could hear my big fish knocking and splashing not far from the edge of the water.

Hemi and I began pulling my big fish in. It was a strong fish, swimming backwards in the shallow water.

'He's swimming backwards!' That's what I remember that Hemi said. Then whoa, we couldn't pull anymore. 'He's found a rock,' said Hemi, 'and he's hanging on by his tail. Hold,' he said. 'But don't pull any more. Go and get us a gaff and a torch,' he said to James.

Hemi and I held on while James ran home for a gaff-hook and a torch.

'If we keep on pulling we could break our line, or break the mouth of your big fish and then we'd never land him.' That's what Hemi said.

James was only a little circle of light and a sound of stones sliding as he came running. He gave the torch and gaff to Hemi, then held the line with me.

My father Hemi walked out just a little way into the water with my sister Tangimoana splashing along behind him. He put the little circle of torch light close to the surface of the sea and gaffed my big fish under its head. He swung his arm round and pulled the big fish free of the rock that it had lashed its tail to.

We hauled it out onto dry shore while it barked and barked and smacked at the stones with its long heavy tail. It is in my memory that the big fish was much much bigger than me, and longer than the little dinghy sitting on the shore.

'We got it, we got it,' Tangimoana was shouting, and there was talking and noise from everyone.

'It's a conger Dad,' James said. 'A big conger.'

'It's bigger than he is,' said Hemi, 'Boyboy it's bigger than you.'

We dragged the big eel up further onto the beach and my father Hemi found a heavy piece of wood and whacked my big fish on the head with it. I do remember the sound. My brother Manu was hiding away with Mary's arms round him, and she was saying, 'Never you matter Boy. Mary look after Boy.'

My father Hemi lifted the big eel from under its gills and half-slid half-carried it to the verandah where we could see it in the light. It was half the length of the verandah, or that's what I remember. It was shiny and black, and shiny silver underneath. Its eyes were little dark pips, and you could tell nothing from its eyes – nothing about its life or its death. Its head was the size of my head, or that's what I remember. And I remember that I was both sorry for my fish and glad about it. Also I remember that I was not afraid of it even though you could tell nothing from its eyes.

We pulled out the stomach of my big fish, and the cocka-bullies and crabs that it had been feeding on. Then Hemi cut off its head that was as big as my own head, or that's how I remember it. He made a long cut down the middle of it, from its head to its tail, then took the long bone out and opened the fish out flat. The whiteness of the inside was a surprise to me.

Hemi sent Tangi for the salt and James for the tub. I helped James to hose out the tub, then we poured the salt into it. The pile of salt was like a little snow mountain and when we put the water in, the little snow mountain melted right away. Hemi and Roimata cut the eel into strips and put the strips into the brine we had made. Hemi scrubbed a heavy board to cover the tub with so that the fish would stay clean, and so that cats would not come and try to take the fish away.

Well we were up late that night helping with my big fish, that's what I remember, and we hadn't even had our baths by then. We had to hurry and not play in the bath, and not be a big eel swimming and splashing.

Manu got into my bed so that he wouldn't call out and cry in the night. We went right under the blankets and we were big conger eels living under the water at the base of the snow mountain. We had little eyes like pips and long fins from head to tail. We had sharp close-together teeth and crabs in our bellies, and we swam and dived and fought and bit and flopped our tails until all the blankets were on the floor.

Then our mother Roimata came in to speak to us and to tidy us, but still we did not go to sleep for a long time after that. I don't remember if Manu cried in the night, and called and kicked and struggled in the dark. I don't remember if that was one of the nights that I woke with his fingers pinching hard into my arm.

There is a lot to remember about that night, and some of it is my own remembering, and some of it is from what I have been told since. But what I remember most of all about then, what I remember truly and really was that I *knew*. I knew that there was a big fish for me. I knew when Hemi said that he was going to get herrings, when I went to the shed for the line, when I was lifted into the dinghy, when the water was soft, orange and bangled, when I let the big, heavy line down, when the night came, and the cold came – but I do not really remember the cold – I knew as I listened to the soft sea sounds, and before the pull came, that there was a big fish for me. And what I have known ever since then is that my knowing, my own knowingness, is different. It is a before, and a now, and an after knowing, and not like the knowing that other people have. It is a now knowing as if everything is now. My mother Roimata knows about me. On that night she said to me, 'You knew didn't you, Toko? You knew.'

We were up early the next day and my father and my uncles did not go out fishing early as they had planned. First of all they buried the head of the fish and the insides of the fish at the roots of the passionfruit vine. Then we all went up back into the bush to get green manuka brush for the smoke fire. Hemi started the sweet-smell fire in the smoke drum and we took the eel pieces out of the brine and dabbed the wetness away from them with a cloth. Then Hemi and Uncle Stan hung the pieces in the drum with all the smoke coming up, and they showed James and all of us how to keep the smoke fire going with the manuka without letting any flames happen.

52

So then we had work for the rest of the day looking after the smoke. I don't remember, but I know, that it would have been our brother James who did everything and understood it all and knew what to do. He could always do grown-up things. He could always be careful and patient and tidy, like Hemi, that's what our mother Roimata said.

When Hemi and our uncles came home they were pleased with James and all of us, and they took the strips of eel from the drum.

The eel flesh was goldy and smelled of the sea and the trees. We wanted to eat some of it right then but Hemi was a little angry with us and told us you didn't eat food until it had been shared, especially if it was from the sea. Ours is a big family he said, which was something to always remember.

9

Toko

There is more to the story of when I was five, and it is about when I went to give Granny Tamihana her pieces of fish.

Granny heard me walking on her path. She knew it was me by the special sound of my walking, and she called out, 'Haeremai Tokowaru-i-te-Marama.' I sat down on her door-step to take my boots off, although that is not a rule for me. I am allowed in houses wearing my special boots as long as I wipe them carefully. But I was pleased to get the big boots off and go into Granny's kitchen. Granny wasn't in the kitchen but I knew where she would be. I went through to the little porch of windows where she was seated on her sheepskin rug preparing strips of flax for her baskets.

I held up the bag of fish for her to see and she said that I was very good and strong. That's what I remember. She said I was a good fisherman and a good little father to her, and a good little father to all my family, and that my fish was myself to give. And she said that she was the one that was going to cook the fish in milk for me, and that she and I were going to eat the fish together, soon, at her own table. Soon when her basket was made.

I put the fish into her fridge so that the little cat would not steal. Then the cat and I watched Granny scraping the flax strips and making the muka at the ends. Then she plaited the muka ends together until her work looked like the long bone that Hemi had taken out of my fish.

While she worked she was telling me and showing me which to lift and which to pull but it was too much to remember. It was just as if she was waving her hands – as if she held the flax strips and did a little green dance with her hands, and then after a while there was a new basket for me.

'I make myself,' she said. 'And give it.'

The sun was coming into the little room of windows. I remember feeling warm and happy on one of Granny's rugs with the garden smell of flax and the sea-sound of her voice, and the shifting sounds of her body and her liney hands.

'Here's your basket nearly finish,' she said. 'Make some handles for your basket when we had our kai.'

Perhaps I went to sleep then, or maybe I followed Granny to the kitchen and watched her heating the fish in a pot of milk, and mixing the dough for the paraoa parai and floating the dough pieces in a pan of fat. I remember the two of us sitting at her table with the fish steaming on our plates and syrup melting and running down the sides of our warm bread. I think I remember Granny putting the very tip of her finger on the knob of her teapot lid as she poured tea for us, or else I know it because it's what she always does. I remember that she talked and talked advising me about everything to do with my whole life. Some of the things she told me were not right out of my understanding, but only sitting on the edge of it. Even so my understanding was more than ordinary for a person who was five. Well that's what I've been told. Given in place of a straight body, and to make up for almost drowning – nobody has told me that but I think it might be so.

And I remember Granny getting up from the table and taking the fire poker from where it was hanging on the wall and swinging the fire door of the wood range down. She stooped, and rattled the burning wood so that the sparks danced, and then she poked more wood in. Fire caught the new wood, and the dry manuka bark lifted and curled and flamed. There was rumbling in the chimney like a storm coming.

Then Granny stood, and I thought that she could have come out of the fire, like a magic fire woman. She stood, in her dark dress, with her old, old face and smoke hair. Her eyes had two dark centres but the whites were lined with red like little fiery pathways. And I tried to walk the fiery pathways but found that they led to places where it was difficult to follow. The way along the pathways was too far, and too magic, too secret and too locked away to follow, or that's what I think now.

We washed and dried our dishes and put them away. I shook the tablecloth outside where the seagulls come, then I followed Granny through to the sitting room with its big brown chairs and flowery cushions and photographs in big wooden frames. The photographs were of long-ago people in best clothes. One was of Granny when she was a girl, standing by her brother who had been dead for seventy years. That's what Granny said. 'That's Tokowaru-i-te-Marama, your great-granduncle, and he's been dead for seventy years. Only me and him, you know,' she said, 'the two of us. And after that, only me.'

Back in the little window room I watched Granny make muka and plait the handles for my basket.

'Riding our horses,' she said. 'Only a little time after that photo there, and the tide down low. Galloping, galloping on our horses on the low-tide sand. Well there is a kehua there that day, on that little rock, and that kehua give my brother's horse a very big fright. Yes, the horse see a very big kehua there on the little rock sticking up in the low water just in front of here. Well. The horse get very wild you see, very wild. The horse get a very big fright. My brother fly out in the air you see, because of the big kehua make his horse very wild. And down, down, and splash in the small water. And bang. His head break on that rock there with a big kehua on it. My poor brother, ka pakaru te upoko.

'Those days I cry and cry for my brother. And smack him too. They make my brother all ready for the people to come, and dress him up nice and put him in our wharenui there. And I look at him, and you know I smack him hard. I throw my flowers down hard, and I kick that pretty box with my brother in very, very hard.

'Well my daddy and my aunties growl at me and hold tight on to me, and I can't smack and kick. I have to be a good girl after that. I have to be good, and all the people from all everywhere come and see my poor brother. I have to be a good girl.

'No more fishing for a long time after,' Granny said. 'No

more fishing and no more going in the sea. Just like when you are born, Little Father. All the people have to wait and wait for the water be right again. Just like for you, Little Father.'

She gave me the finished basket which was cool and green-smelling, then she led me back to the photos.

'The time your great-granduncle is born, that's the time all those people die of a bad sickness, tokowaru i te marama. Eight people die in one month here, and eight tupapaku on our marae. Eight in one month. But it's a good name for you Little Father, your great-granduncle's name. And it's your own name now.'

I thought of the other Tokowaru-i-te-Marama galloping along the sand, being thrown from his horse and falling to hit his head on the rock. The dull, hard sound of when my father Hemi whacked my big fish with the heavy stick came back to my mind. And the life of the long-ago Toko and the life of my big fish seemed somehow to come together. There was a big kehua there.

I put on my boots and went home along the beach shoulder-ing the gifts I had been given.

There is something else to do with my five-year-old story and the story of my big fish. It is to do with the passionfruit vine. 'Vine' and 'brine' were both new words to me then, and these words quickly recall that time for me whenever I hear them.

My mother Roimata had taken a passionfruit cutting from Granny Tamihana's vine. At the time when I caught my big fish the cutting was dry and without life, that's what I've been told. But after we buried the fish head and fish guts there the plant began to grow and grow. The branches began to swim everywhere like a multiplication of eels. It was as if the big eel head with its little seed-eyes was birthing out trail after trail of its young. All the little eels swarmed the shed walls and the trees, whipping their tails and latching them to the walls and branches, still growing and multiplying all the time. And the eel-vines had a thousand hidden eyes, a thousand tails and a thousand hidden hearts.

The hearts are dark and warm and fit in the cup of your

57

hand. You can pull out the hearts without pain, and when you open them you find the thousand dark seed-eyes. The seeds are a new beginning, but started from a death. Well everything is like that – that's what my mother Roimata says. End is always beginning. Death is life.

The goldy seeded fruit is sharp-tasting and stinging, and leaves you with red stained fingers and a smarting, blooded mouth.

And the endless vine going everywhere is like a remembrance of the time, which is really a now-time, of when I was five, and of the big barking fish that I knew was waiting for me on the white sky night in the orange lagoon.

10

Hemi

The day the works closed down for good he walked home along the beach leading a horse. It was a good horse, quiet and strong, even if a little old for what he needed.

It had been a very difficult year for a lot of people, with fewer and fewer jobs and so many people out of work. It had been a time of stoppages and strikes, and so much unrest, and now he was out of work too. Well, he was glad. He was sorry about the general hardships that people were facing, but for himself, for the whanau, he was glad. He had important things to do, things that had been on his mind for years now, and he'd done nothing but talk about it. A bit old for it now, he wondered? Well he was always a little slow getting onto things, inclined always to wait for things to happen. Should have been on with it before now, for the sake of the ones without work wanting to return home. But anyway now was the time.

It was more than thirty years ago, at fifteen, that he'd left school to work the land when his father died. He'd had to take much of the responsibility for the gardens then, while his older brother Stan was away getting further education and his cousins were doing their trades. His own apprentice-ship, his own education, had been on the land, and after his father had died Grandfather Tamihana had taught him everything to do with planting, tending, gathering, storing and marketing. He'd been taught about the weather and seasons, the moon phases and the rituals to do with growing. At the same time he was made aware that he was being given knowledge on behalf of a people, and that they all trusted him with that knowledge. It wasn't only for him but for the family.

They'd had a reasonable living for a number of years with

he and his grandfather doing most of the work, and others helping when they could. Then the old man died, and once his brother, sisters and cousins married and began building homes and having families there had not been enough in it for survival, and not enough people free to work in the gardens.

He had not been happy about giving up what he knew was a charge that he'd been given. But it had only been given up temporarily, he'd always known that. He'd always known that one day he would return to the land, and that the land would support them all again.

And they still had their land, that was something to feel good about. Still had everything, except for the hills. The hills had gone, but that was before his time and there was nothing he could do about that, nothing anyone could do. What had happened there wasn't right but it was over and done with. Now, at least, the family was still here, on the ancestral land. They still had their urupa and their wharenui, and there was still clean water out front.

It hadn't always been easy either. They'd had to watch, be careful over the years. There had been requests to the family to sell land at the back, and some pressure on them to open up the road along the beach. But they'd all resisted firmly over a number of years. Just as well.

These days people were looking more to their land. Not only to their land, but to their own things as well. They had to if they didn't want to be wiped off the face of the earth. There was more determination now – determination which had created hope, and hope in turn had created confidence, and energy. Things were stirring, to the extent of people fighting to hold onto a language that was in danger of being lost, and to the extent of people struggling to regain land that had gone from them years before. The people at Te Ope were an example and it was looking good for the Te Ope people now. They were going to win their struggle at last, after years and years of letter-writing and delegations and protest. It was only since the people decided on occupation that attention had been given to their situation and an enquiry had been brought about. Te Ope was going to win through now that the courts had found them to be right in what they had always claimed, and had made a decision in their favour.

Good on them. It was things like that that made you feel good. He was proud that he and his family, the whole whanau, had given support to the Te Ope people. Well it was no distance for them to go with their koha, and Tangimoana, James and other young ones had spent many weekends there over the past two years or so. That was something to be proud of, and anyway it was right they should give their support. After all they had their own connections there, their own whanaunga. It was right, no getting away from it.

The young ones had not only given their help and support but they'd learned some good things too. One more legal battle to go then Te Ope would be building, rebuilding their wharenui on their own land at last. Had their plans drawn up already, that's how confident they were, and they'd asked James to come and help with the carvings of their house. Well that was a great thing. There'd always been carvers among their tipuna here, but although the works and the stories had survived, the skills had not. Now, through James, and thanks to an old man at Te Ope, they would get those skills back into the family again. It was meant, everything was meant, and people hadn't forgotten how to care. Much had been lost, but people hadn't stopped knowing how to care for each other. It was good. He aha te mea nui i te ao? He tangata, he tangata, he tangata. He believed in it.

And people were looking to their land again. They knew that they belonged to the land, had known all along that there had to be a foothold otherwise you were dust blowing here there and anywhere – you were lost, gone. It was good there was more focus on it now, and more hope.

For him, being out of a job meant that he would be able to get on with his real work, and that he'd be able to pass on what he'd been given. Everything was meant, that's what he'd always believed. But if you missed the signs, or let yourself be side-tracked, you could lose out. Everything was meant but you had to do your bit too.

The two young ones had seen him coming with the horse. They'd be disappointed that it wasn't a riding horse, but it was good to have a horse again. There was a good horse smell to do with the land, and there was a good whiff of the sea mingling with it. He could give Manu and Toko a ride, then he'd have to go and finish the fence he'd been making. There was plenty of time now to get everything in shape, and there'd be plenty of help too. There were young ones here with no work to go to, who were looking forward to doing something that was their own, for themselves. There were those who had moved away but who would come back as they got sent down the road from their jobs. James would spend time here and time at Te Ope, getting some of those other skills back into the family. He'd come home when he was needed. Tangi would go to university because it was what the people wanted her to do. She'd be home with them in the holidays.

They'd have to make sure that they were producing enough for their own kai first, and for any manuhiri of course. Wouldn't be easy. Then later there'd be surplus to sell or store. They'd try out some new crops, the markets were different now. Couldn't wait to get into it.

'What's his name?' Manu was steadying Toko with his arm. They'd been hurrying. 'You'll have to think of a name.'

'Didn't he have a name before?'

'Didn't ask his name, we'll have to give him one.'

'Well can we ride him?'

'Not a riding horse but you can have a ride. He's a working horse.'

He helped Manu on to the horse, then lifted Toko and seated him in front.

'He needs a big name,' Toko was saying.

'Call him Kaha then.'

Kaha. Yes, it was a good name, strong but gentle. Manu had the knack. He always knew the special thing about a person – or a horse. 'Kia kaha,' he said, moving the horse forward again.

Roimata was waiting for them on the verandah.

'What do you think of him, Roi?'

'Big. Bigger than the one you used to have.'

'This one's a worker.'

'Cold mornings when you'd been hurrying your horse to school you'd see her steaming.'

Years ago.

Manu slid down the horse's flank and onto the verandah. Hemi lifted Toko down and steadied him. 'We'll take him out the back and find something to put water in,' he said, 'Then we'll have to finish that fence before it gets dark. Kia kaha.'

Pigtail girl. Waiting there every morning holding the gate of the school paddock open for them. And so good to Mary always, he'd never forget. None of them would ever forget that. A couple of years later, she was six or seven, was when her father started bringing her there to the beach. Not long after her mother died. Must have been a lonely pair in those days, but he hadn't thought about it then. A good man, her father. Good to them during the war years. He'd come there and given their old people a hand in the gardens at a time when there were no young men about. If there was a death, or a wedding, he'd be there to help.

Just like another uncle. And Roimata was just like another cousin to all of them. Never thought then that he'd be married to her one day, but she knew. She said that she knew when she was five that she'd marry him. Well he was a real slow arse but he supposed it was all meant. Couldn't imagine a life with anyone else, even if it was true that there had been someone else in his life for a while.

Couldn't remember where he'd met Sue, but it was probably at a party. At the rugby club, most likely. He seemed to be in love with her, really in love. Then. But looking back now it was easy to see that he and Sue were really nothing to do with each other. That was what Granny Tamihana had said at the time too. She'd told him that he couldn't just see a woman at a dance and marry her, someone who was nothing to do with him, or with anything of his. Anyone else wouldn't have listened to old Granny and her growling, and he hadn't wanted to at first. But he had listened, and he did know, he'd really known all along. Sue knew it too. They'd both known that he'd never leave there, that he'd never leave his sister

Mary, or his mother who was ill by then. And Sue wouldn't have fitted into their household, they both knew it.

Well he'd felt very lonely after Sue left and he'd thought he'd never marry. Not that he hadn't wanted to, but it was the way things were. He couldn't turn his back on them.

Then Roimata came. She'd been a part of their lives, she and her father. But she'd left there when she was fifteen, the same age as Tangimoana was now. In some things he was a man by then, with a man's load. Roimata was like a young cousin going away. Not that he'd forgotten her, but it was Mary who'd noticed it most when Roimata left. It was Mary who had missed her.

He hadn't known then that Roimata would come back twelve years later looking for him. Funny though, because when she did come, when he saw her, he knew . . . as if he'd been waiting. . . . It was all meant, he supposed.

Back from the house he began work on the almost completed fence. The next day he would sort out all the gear that was hanging in the shed. Didn't think there'd be too many repairs needed, perhaps a bit of rust to deal with, but they had looked after it all these years. They'd clear the ground out back first, then start ploughing. He was looking forward to that first furrow, that first turn of the soil. Before winter they'd get their firewood down from the hills. Couldn't beat a horse when it came to getting manuka off the slopes.

And there were so many things in his head at the moment. It wasn't just the gardens, it was everything, the whole place, the people. There was the sea. It was true that they'd always used the sea, and the shores, but they were not using them to the same extent now as they had earlier. The kids knew a lot already. They were good in the water, and in the boats, but there was more that the young ones could be shown now that there was time, and freedom. It was important now, important for their survival. There were all the things about the moons and tides, winds and currents, and how to find the fishing grounds, that needed to be told. Not just told but shown. There were skills like net mending and crayfish-pot making that needed to be passed on.

Then apart from the land and sea, apart from the survival

things, there were their songs and their stories. There was their language. There would be more opportunity now to make sure that they, the older ones, handed on what they knew.

Kids were different these days. They wanted knowledge of their own things, their own things first. They were proud and didn't hide their culture, and no one could bullshit them either.

In his day they had been expected to hide things, to pretend they weren't what they were. It was funny how people saw each other. Funny how you came to see yourself in the mould that others put you in, and how you began not to believe in yourself. You began to believe that you should hide away in the old seaweed like a sand flea, and that all you could do when disturbed was hop about and hope you wouldn't get stood on. But of course you did get stood on.

Well their ancestors had been rubbished in schools, and in books, and everywhere. So were their customs, so was their language. Still were rubbished too, as far as he could see. Rubbished or ignored. And if those things were being rubbished then it was an attack on you, on a whole people. You could get weak under the attack, then again you could become strong.

The kids these days were strong, well some of them were. Others were lost and without hope. But the strong ones? They were different, tougher than what his lot had been as kids. They didn't accept some of the messages they were receiving about themselves, couldn't afford to if they wanted to stay on the face of the earth.

Education was a good thing, he'd always believed that, wanted it for the kids. And the kids believed it. But the kids wouldn't take any rubbish, and that made sense. Didn't know what was wrong with them all in his day. They went into everything blind trying to find a pathway to heaven. Believed everything they were told about themselves, accepted every humiliation as though it was good for them.

There were exceptions even in his day of course, like their mate Reuben up in Te Ope, same age as himself. At the time when he himself was working the land, learning what he could, Reuben was standing up to them all, digging his toes in. Years of his young life, and all on his own at first. But Reuben had never taken any crap and had never taken old people for fools the way the authorities had. It was true that young and old had had quite bad disagreements at times over the handling of things, but Reuben had always had his head on straight. No doubts. Always believed in himself and his people.

His own daughter Tangi was like that too, never let anyone put her or her people down. Had such a clear view of what she stood for and nothing got past her. If she'd been round in Reuben's day she'd have been up there beside him spitting. Yes Tangimoana was the one. He hoped his daughter wouldn't suffer too much for the sort of person she was.

The night she was born was the worst night of his whole life. The little one had come without too much trouble, but then there had been difficulty with the afterbirth and his Roimata had come near to death. When he saw her there so colourless and unmoving after the emergency operation he felt as though he'd killed her.

Hadn't wanted any more kids after that, but after a few years Roimata had decided to have another. She was all right that time, but it was little Manu who'd had to fight for his life, spending his first few weeks in an incubator. Well perhaps those first few weeks would be the only time Manu would ever spend separated from the family, time would tell. You had to trust what people knew in their hearts. People knew things in their hearts, even little kids, or especially little kids. Manu knew he shouldn't go to school, and their decision to keep him home turned out good for all of them. They'd had to decide what was important and what was not.

After Manu they'd decided not to have any more kids. And he had decided to go and have something done about it himself. Wasn't so straightforward those days either. Well everything was meant, but that didn't mean you just sat round and hoped. The old aunties had had him on about it too of course, but it was just their way of bringing it all out in the open, letting him know they were backing him up in what he'd done, letting him know they thought he had good enough reason. His business, but as usual it was the whole family's business.

So then Toko was a real gift. That wasn't what they'd thought at first of course, because they'd been upset and angry at the time. Angry wasn't the word for it. He'd felt like killing . . . someone. Didn't know who and could only guess. They'd never found out from Mary, who had no memory or understanding of what they'd been asking her, and it seemed she had no memory of the baby's birth either. He'd never forget the way she'd looked that night when he got home. No expression, nothing to say. And he'd never forget the poor crooked little baby they'd shown him.

That old bloke had never turned up again, lucky for him, but still you could only guess. And what they had not thought of at first was that it could have been . . . Mary. Her own . . . desire. But even so she was done wrong.

And they'd tried to trace him at first, Williams. They'd found out that he had a little house up the line that he lived in during the winter months, but the house was empty when he and Stan had gone there. Neighbours had been able to tell them that the old fella took to the roads and beaches every year in the late spring and that he'd been gone a week. Then not long after that they'd seen in the paper where he'd been found dead on the side of the road somewhere.

God he'd been upset at the time. He still felt guilty about it, not angry any more but guilty, after having promised his mother that he'd always look after Mary. Well they'd named the old bloke as father anyway, whether he was responsible or not. Joseph Williams.

Hadn't known his name until they'd been told it by neighbours. And yet Mary – it almost seemed as though she'd known it. Then they'd read about Joseph Williams in the newspaper. There'd been quite a write-up about him too.

Anyway Toko was something special they'd been given, no doubt about it, Joseph Williams or no Joseph Williams. A taniwha. That's what they'd been given, a taniwha, who somehow gave strength . . . and joy to all of them.

And he himself had been given a lot, and now that he was at last getting back to the family things he could deserve what

67

he'd been given. You had to deserve things. He was getting back to it and it was a good feeling.

It was dark now, on this, his first day of no work, and he wouldn't get the fence finished after all, but there was tomorrow. The fence was good enough as it was to keep the horse from getting out. He could hear it snuffling and stamping in the dark, and he could see the darker-than-black shadow of it as he made his way, first to the shed with the gear, and then to the house. He could hear Mary in the house singing.

11

Roimata

The week we learned of the closing down of Hemi's job was a time of some anxiety for me, as it was for many people. I wondered what we would do, how we would live. But when I spoke to Hemi he only said, 'Everything we need is here.' He then began to retell his story, so that the children came and listened.

He told again of how it had been once, and I was able to see the land again as it had been, and saw people who were gone by then, stooping into the soil. One of them was my father. There was dark earth which seemed to sit darkly under dark skies. And then as the earth greened, and the green thickened and spread, the skies lightened into broad summers. That was how it seemed in memory.

Bags of potatoes, kumara and carrots were loaded onto the truck, bags that I had often helped Mary and her mother and other members of the family to stitch with a needle and string. Or there were boxes of tomatoes and cabbages and corn to be shared or taken away for sale. I saw myself with the other children carrying pumpkins, as though each of us had snared a sun in the circle of our arms.

And Hemi told the new story too, of how it would be again, of how the land could be brought back into full production using new crops that he had already tried out in the house garden and already knew something about. The final payments from the job would help us get started, he said. He wanted to work a horse again but to have a small tractor and truck as well. As he spoke I felt how full of hope and confidence he was. *

It was one day during the spring of the new gardens that Toko came hurrying in to speak to me. We had told and written

69

our stories that morning then gone out to help in the gardens. In the early afternoon my sister-in-law and I had returned to the wharekai to prepare lunch.

Toko hurried in after us. 'The stories are changing,' he said. His eyes were wide and bright and his hair hung damply about his face.

'Don't hurry so much,' I said.

'When are they coming?' he asked.

'Who? When are who coming?'

'All the people. The people that we make the gardens for.'

'The gardens are for us, for our kai . . . and for the market.'

'And for people.'

'There'll always be kai . . . for people . . . for our visitors.'

'When will they come? Are they coming soon?'

'I don't know.' I didn't know what else to say. I only knew that Tokowaru had a special knowing.

Then he said, 'Will they stamp their feet and march and run? Will their eyes shine green, yellow and silver? Will they be sore-footed with bands on their heads? What will they hold in their hands?'

I didn't know how to answer him.

'And will their hunger and anger be hard?' he said. 'What will they do and what will we do? Will we feed them and help them? And will they help us too? Will they do it for me, or you? Will my sister be with them, and my brother? Will our fathers be there, or our children? Will it be us? What will it be? Is it for me?'

'I don't know, I don't know!' I couldn't say any more than that. I could only hold him close to me, holding him, fearing him, as I had held and feared him on the day that he was born.

12

Toko

There's a story about Te Ope. Part of the story is old and part of it is new. The old part of the story has been told to us by my second mother Roimata. The new part has been told in the newspapers and on television in words and pictures. But also we have been to Te Ope and we have seen the new story for ourselves, and we have been part of the new story too. My brother James and my sister Tangimoana stay at Te Ope sometimes, and when they come home Manu and I listen excitedly to all the stories they bring.

The old story is about an area of Te Ope land where the old Te Ope families lived. There were twenty-five houses that people lived in and an empty house that was used as a wharenui. It was not a whare whakairo like the house that we have here, but just an ordinary house where a family had once lived. It had had some walls taken out of it and had been dedicated by the families as a wharenui.

There was a small orchard behind the houses, and the hills behind the orchard were covered in scrub. The people who lived there were poor and could not develop the land, but they grew their own food and had plenty of firewood for their stoves and fireplaces. They were like us now, not having any work, but they were much more poor than we are now and had a very hard life, that's what Roimata said. And they did not have the sea like we have. But they were not poor in some things, and whatever they had they shared. There was no town there like there is now.

Then later the war came. This was the long-ago war. Not my grandfather's war but my great-grandfather's war where the soldiers waded through mud, and the shells came clouting them, knocking them flat so that they died with mud in their mouths. Their friends who were not dead used the dead bodies for bridges so that they could crawl to somewhere safe, or used them to step on, or just to hold on to. It's all in the stories. They were red and black days with mud and blood, with shell explosion and rifle fire and dying. The men still alive walked back to life on the backs of the people dead.

There were no young men at Te Ope because they had all gone to war. But the country wanted more than Te Ope's young men. They wanted the land for purposes of war, and because their land was in a good place, because there was a good flat area there, it was very suitable. That is what was told to the people of Te Ope at the time, the land was very suitable. But it has been said since that this was an excuse to scatter the people, destroy their homes, and take the land.

The people quietly packed up and went to the state houses that had been rented to them. They were to return to the land when it was no longer needed for purposes of war. They went quietly because they were poor, that's what Roimata said.

The people of Te Ope did not expect to go past their land one day and see that their houses had gone. But when they went to find out about their houses they were told that the land could not be used as a landing field if it had houses on it. The houses were derelict anyway, they were told, and not fit to be lived in. They had been given better houses, they were told.

The people agreed that they had been given better houses, except that the houses had not really been given. These houses did not belong to them but to the government and they paid rent to live in them. To pay rent was difficult for most because there was still no work for them. There was no land for gardens and no wood for their fires. These houses were scattered everywhere so that the family was separated, and also they didn't have their meeting-house any more.

But that wasn't a proper meeting-house, they were told. No carvings, no nothing, and it was falling down anyway. They couldn't possibly call that a meeting-house, they needn't try and put that one across. And what did they mean their family was separated? Each family had been given a house, a bigger and better house than the one they had come from,

72

they should be grateful, and right in the city too. If you really wanted a job you could find one. If you really wanted a garden what's to stop you? That's what they were told.

The Te Ope people talked until there was no more use in talking and then they went back to their scattered city houses that did not belong to them. They did not have anything that belonged to them any more except that they had each other, scattered as they were, and they had their stories.

Also they had an old man called Rupena who wrote letters. He wasn't greatly old then, not greatly old like our old mother Tamihana, but was a man whose family had grown up, and whose sons were away at war. He wrote letters setting out all that had been promised and all that had been done, and what the people wanted. No one knew about the letters except for a few members of the family and those who had received them. The letters were a part of the old story.

They later became a part of the new story, but the old man was dead by then, though not long dead. My father Hemi remembers him and my mother Roimata too. He was helped down from the bus and across the sacred ground when our mother Roimata returned here. That was when our own kuia died, mother of our father, but it was before we were born. There were white seagulls flying, and white waves. The old man's hair was white against the dark clothes that people wore, and when he stood to speak he said that our grand-mother, lying in her coffin in the glinting house, was a singing bird and a soul of joy. That's what Roimata has told us.

The new story began at about the time when our mother was a girl and when our father left school to work the gardens, which was more than thirty years after the beginning of the old story. Reuben of Te Ope, grandson of Rupena, was six-teen then. One day he went home from school and said to his parents, 'I'm not going there any more.' His mother and father were angry and told him not to talk that way. They told him he was to go back to school and that was that, no arguing. 'But what for? What for?' he kept asking.

'You must have a good job,' they said. 'You must have a decent life. For your future,' they said.

'I can get a job,' he said. 'And I do have a decent life.' But

73

they wouldn't listen to him. 'You'll be out on the streets, like your brother, jobless and pohara, not bothering to come home, feeling ashamed. You'll be like some of your cousins, drunk and useless. You'll end up in jail.'

'It doesn't mean that. Leaving school doesn't mean that.'

'That's what it means. We've seen it. You can't leave.'

'Well what about both of you? Yous didn't stay at school. Hardly went to school . . .'

'It was different . . . We had to and . . . couldn't afford, but you. . . .'

'You're making me eat shit sending me back there.'

'Now look, you don't need to . . . you're going back. Because we know . . . and the old man and them, they know too. They know about no work, and their homes falling down about them, about people helpless. . . .'

'If their houses fell down there was still the land,' Reuben said.

'We're not talking about the houses on the land that were pulled down, we're talking about the houses after that. Fell down. And anyway that was then, that's not now.'

'But why isn't it? Why not now?'

'Well that's an old story, you know as well as we do.'

'I do. I know the story and I know the place. You, both of yous, and him, the old man, you took me there to run in the finals. And he told me. "This is your land," he said. "This is the place," and he told me all the things he'd told before, but he pointed here and he pointed there. "We tried, you know," he said to me. "Me and my sisters and some of our cousins," and he said some of their names. He told me who. "We went back and back," he told me. "We wrote," that's what he told me. I listened to him. . . .'

'Well listen to him now. Get on over to Aunty's and talk to him. He's the one. He'll talk sense into you. Tell you to stick at school, make something of yourself.'

'Aren't I something already? Aren't I? That's all I learn at school – that I'm not somebody, that my ancestors were rubbish and so I'm rubbish too. That's all I learn from the newspapers, that I'm nobody, or I'm bad and I belong in jail. You're telling me that now too.'

74

'It's not that, Son. It's not what we mean. You've got the brains. You should use them.'

'I am. That's what I'm doing right now, using my brains. I've thought about it, I tell you. I've already thought. And what I know is I'm not learning one thing, not one thing, that's anything to do with me, or us. And some of the stuff, well, it's against me and against us. It makes us dumb, it puts us wrong.'

'But it gets you somewhere.'

'Where somewhere?'

'Somewhere. It gets a future for you.'

'But that's eating shit.'

'Work's not eating shit. . . .'

'Sometimes. . . .'

'It's keeping your neck out of the water, you know, not . . . drowning. But it can be more. For you. You can do anything. You know . . . anything you want, can't you see?'

'You'll make me go there and eat shit.'

'You don't go back and it's like you're throwing shit in our faces.'

'You've been shoved into it anyway, you don't even know. . . .'

'Don't get smart and don't argue. You finish the year off then see. . . .'

'See?'

'Just to the end of the year, Son. You've done good so far and you might as well.'

So Reuben returned to school because he couldn't get his parents to understand. It was his Mum and Dad who told all this to Roimata, but that was later.

Reuben did go to see his grandfather Rupena, and asked what he should do. The old man didn't answer Reuben's questions about school, but he said, 'Don't go out on the streets, go on the land. Our land, yours. Belongs to all of us, all of yous.' Then he said, 'Get the letters, in the wardrobe. Only copies. Copied the ones I sent. Read them and then you'll know. Show your cousins and then all of yous will know us old ones tried, we had a go. You show them we really tried and they won't blame. And if yous can do something . . . well good on yous.'

It was when he got the letters that Reuben began to learn the things that he wanted to learn. Before that no one had known, or hadn't remembered about the copies of the letters that the old man had kept, along with the few replies that he had received.

The first letter had been written after the pulling down of the houses.

'. . . we the people of Te Ope ask you if it was a right thing to take down these houses belonging to us. We think it would be right to talk of these matters first so that we can give our explanations to you and you can give your explanations to us. We write to say why have you done this? We have come to see you but you have only told us it is necessary and quickly gone away leaving us to look at each other. What manner is that? It is too late now, you have taken our houses down. You have taken the timber away. For what reason? You say that these are not good houses. You say that we live in better houses now. That is the truth. But these houses belong to the government and not to the people of Te Ope.

'I will tell you that the meeting-house was blessed in a Christian manner in the name of God who is above all men. But now it is taken down. Why have the blessed timbers been burnt?

'When will this war be ended so that our friends will return to us? But there will be no houses for them, and no gardens to feed them. There will be no house of mourning where we can gather when they bring home the shadows of the dead. Our land will come back to us and then we must build our houses again, but our money is going away to pay our rent.

'These are our thoughts and what do you reply to all of us. . . .'

'As has been already explained the houses of which you speak were demolished because the land is required for a landing field. Since the houses of which you write were substandard I am sure you will agree that there has been no great loss to you. You must appreciate that the homes that have been

76

allotted to you and the other families have been given at a very low rental.

'I note that in your letter you have mentioned a meeting-house. There was no building on the land that could in any way fit such a description. I suggest that you keep strictly to facts if in future you feel you need to make further represent-ations to this office. . . .'

When Reuben finished school he began to study law, but in the evenings and at weekends he would talk about the land and the letters, to his parents and his brother. He would visit the homes of his relatives, or go looking for his cousins in the different parts of town, or in other parts of the country. He showed the letters to all of them so that they were able to discuss them.

After the first letter there was a space of over a year to the second.

'. . . we see that you do not use the land. Why have we, the Maori people of Te Ope, given up our land and our houses when you do not use the land for purposes of war or for any purpose? When will the air base be built because the land is clear now? All of the houses have gone, the trees have been chopped. If you think that the land is not right after all, then we, the people of Te Ope will want to go back there and make our gardens again. We will build up our houses. We will wait there for our sons when this trouble is finished. . . .'

There were other letters like this one belonging to these early years, but there were no replies.

It was before the second war, my grandfather's war, that the land had been made into a playing-field by men on relief work. There was only one letter from that time, telling of how the promise had been broken.

'. . . the land has not been used as an air base or for any purpose of war. We have come there to you but you only look into your books. You say that you will speak to this one and that one. We go away, we come back, but still there is no reply to us.

'Now you send men to make a park there while we of Te Ope only watch and do nothing because we do not have houses there any more. When will this stop? The park must stop.

Return the Te Ope people to their land.'

There was a short reply to this letter saying that the office would look into the matter, but that was all.

The people later gave copies of the letters to us so that we would all know their stories, but that was before I was born. Later Roimata and Manu and I made little books with them, and read them and told them over and over.

And we made a big book from the newspaper cuttings that our Aunty had saved too. They were from the time when Reuben went to live on the land. They were pictures and stories of the young Reuben and the people who supported him, and pictures and stories of the park and playing-field and the clubrooms. There were stories and pictures of arrests and people going to court, and stories of family picnics that Reuben had organised for the people, and pictures of the tents and gardens. Roimata wrote the dates on the pages of our book for us so we would know.

When Reuben was twenty-one he left his studies and went to live on the land. He had talked to people because he wanted them to go with him, but it was only his girlfriend Hiria and his cousin Henry who went with him to stay. His grandfather Rupena, who was old by then and becoming frail, went to support them when he could.

His parents, and other older people of Te Ope, had not wanted Reuben to leave his studies. They did not agree with his way of doing things. But all that Reuben would say to them was, 'He told me to go and live on the land. That's what I'm doing. He supports me and that's all I need.'

'There are other ways, you don't need. . . .'

'He tried the other ways and they treated him as though he was simple. They called him a liar.'

'But it might be different now,' they said.

'It won't be different, and each year will only make it harder.'

'And you can't win. You end up nowhere in the end.'

'He says the land belongs to me, but he means to all of us. I believe him. Should I believe him and do nothing? "Go and live on the land," he says. "Go on the land or you're out on the street." He means all of us.'

'He's old. . . .'

'He told me . . . that's good enough.'

So Reuben went to live on the land and he said that he would never leave the land again. There were newspaper photos of the camp that he set up there, and of others that came, after a while, to join him. There were pictures of Reuben being arrested and of him going quietly away. But others had come to help by then, and after he had been taken away they would move in to take his place, to keep his place warm, that's what they said. Most were of our race but some were not.

Gradually the older people began to give support to Reuben because they all knew that what he was saying was true. They had always known that the land had been taken, that there had been no payments except for rents being cheaper, that letters had been written, that homes and a dedicated house had been pulled down. They knew that the land had been taken for a purpose and not used for that purpose, and had not been returned to them as promised. They knew that they still owned the land. They were ashamed not to support him.

But there were some who continued to be angry and were embarrassed by the trouble he was causing. They said it was too late, it was all in the past, that all the trouble would be for nothing and that land was for everybody. The way it was now, as a park, it could be used by everyone, that's the way of aroha they said. They said that Reuben was a young man who had forgotten, or did not know about the ways of aroha. Some said he wanted the land for himself, and that he was making himself a chief when he was only a child.

Reuben's reply was that while many other people had their own marae, a common place, a good way of connecting the past with the future, they themselves were just blowing in the wind. He told them that it was not true that he knew nothing of aroha, and that if they did all have something that they could share, then they would be able to share it. He was not doing it for himself but for everyone. 'We want land for our meeting-house and our marae. We want the houses back on the land so that people can live on their own land again, die there if they want to. Those people in the past – they left on the understanding that they would return. That understanding still holds, but we now have to force our return. All we are doing is returning to our land, there's no wrong in that.'

The first camp was set up in a corner, out of the way of those who used the park, but many people were angry. In our scrapbook we have all the angry letters from people who wrote to the papers wanting the tents, Reuben and his group, moved. Later there were some letters as well that supported what he was doing, but not at first. There were reports and photos too.

A reporter told Reuben what one of his uncles had said when interviewed – that Reuben was trying to make himself a chief when he was only a child.

'It's true that I am only a child,' Reuben said, 'but it's not true that I want to be a chief. I want those elders that you speak of, my uncle who said it, to support me and lead me. I want them to come here and be my pakeke. The old man's not strong now . . . can't be here all the time. He was the one who told me . . . and he's with me even if they're not.'

It was not Reuben's Mum and Dad who had said that Reuben was trying to be a chief, but they had not supported him either. It was the next day, after they had read what the papers said, that they arrived at the park with a caravan and belongings. They later told all this to Roimata and Hemi, but it was in a newspaper story too.

Although Reuben and some of the others had been arrested by this time, no evidence had been found to show that what they were saying wasn't true so they were soon back on the land again. They were asked to remove their tents and belongings from the area, and they were promised that if they did the matter would be looked into. But they wouldn't move.

When they made their first garden they put it in a place which did not cause trouble to the people using the park. It was a large park and their camp and garden was away in a far corner. One of our pictures showed children watering silverbeet and cabbage plants. But the garden caused a lot of anger. There were angry people, Roimata said, who called the garden destruction and wilful vandalism. But the little garden, she told us, was beautiful, and when they all went there to take their koha and their aroha there were vegetables ready for picking. I was not born then, but it is all in my mind like a memory.

Other attempts were made to get Reuben to shift from the land. In our book there is a picture of the mayor talking to Reuben. 'Mayor Supports Protest' the headline said. It told about the mayor of those days promising to do everything he could and to look into the matter, personally it said, and to discuss the matter with councillors, but first of all Reuben and the others must move themselves and all their things. Then the mayor would support Reuben. Reuben told the mayor that they would be pleased to have his support, but if it meant that they must leave before support was given then they would do without the support. He would never leave the land, he said. And he told the mayor that they were not land protesters, but that they were just people living their lives on land that belonged to them.

Another picture showed how one of Reuben's uncles was sent to the park to ask Reuben to move. But the uncle was told by Reuben's father to go away and to come back with his koha and a blanket. 'Elder Told – Return With Food and Bed' the headline said.

Several times the camp was attacked by angry people. A tent was torn down in the middle of the night, plants were pulled from the gardens and scattered. Rubbish was tipped at the tent openings, a bottle was thrown, glass was scattered on the ground.

But the group had not been shown to be wrong in saying the land belonged to them. More and more support began to be given from all round the country. Many people of our race and many not of our race went there with gifts of food and money. A few stayed, others moved backwards and for- wards as my brother and sister did later, but the struggle had been won by then. There were ten or more people, in three tents and a caravan, who stayed permanently.

Some people were angry about the washing hanging out to dry – towels, shirts, overalls and underwear – out on the tent ropes, and some on lines that had been put up. There was a picture of the washing, and there were words saying 'Washing Offends'. But it was no different from anyone else's washing hanging out on their properties. That's what the papers reported that Reuben's mother had said.

The police were criticised for not taking Reuben and the others away, but there was not much they could do.

Then one day there was a picnic. One Saturday, Reuben and the others living on the land arranged a picnic for family and friends. About two hundred people went there with food and blankets and guitars. They had karakia first, with prayers and hymns. Then they spread the blankets on the playing-fields and sat down with the food and guitars. They had a concert too, using the stand as a stage. There was a big photo of a group in the stand singing and dancing, and other photos of people watching and clapping. 'Stand Staged', the headline said.

But the cricket people who came to play were angry, and that was when the police all came back again and arrested lots of people, taking them away in a bus. There was a photo of the arrested people singing in the bus, and of the people who had not been arrested waving and cheering for the arrested ones. Reuben and his parents, and the others who had been living on the land, had left the grounds before the police came in so that they would not be arrested, and so that they could return to their camp later in the day.

It was not long after this that the full enquiry was begun about the land.

It was because of the enquiry that all of old Rupena's letters came forward, not the copies given to Reuben by the old man, but the ones that he had actually sent, and some of the replies as well, but not all of the replies. They were the letters that a lot of people said didn't really exist, but now they had been found. There was also a letter telling about the taking over of the land, telling how the land would be used and saying how the people would be given housing cheaply in return. The houses at cheap rent were in return for using the land. Using. But there was nothing in that letter about the pulling down of houses. No payments had been made. It was all as old Rupena had said. The land still belonged to the people just as Reuben and his family knew it did. And at last the court of enquiry showed it too.

But what about the sports people and their lease? They had a lease of the land, they said. But Reuben's father said, 'I don't think so. We the owners of the land do not have any agreement with you regarding lease. We the owners of the land have never received any rents or payments of any sort for our land, and this has been shown by the courts.' These are some of the things Reuben's father said. He told these things to Hemi and Roimata, and they were reported in the paper too.

There was excitement and joy among the people of Te Ope when the court of enquiry showed them as right, but their struggle wasn't ended. There had been improvements, the courts decided. There were playing-fields, clubrooms and a stand. The land is yours, the courts said, but not the improvements. You will have to pay for the improvements, and they were told an amount of money that was impossible for them to pay.

After that the people were offered money for the land. This caused more upset among the Te Ope people. Some wanted to sell because they felt they could never use the land. Others said the land was theirs and always had been, and that they were going to occupy it and build their whare whakairo there. They were already planning their carved meeting-house as well as the homes they wanted to build. Quarrels began again among the people, some saying that those who wanted to sell were interested only in money. But those who wanted to sell said that the others were all trying to be chiefs, and were really wanting the land for themselves.

More quarrels and unhappiness came about when a compromise was made. Those occupying the land, along with their lawyer, worked out the value of the houses and the price that they thought should have been paid to the people, along with compensation for gardens and trees that had been removed. They worked out what families had paid in rents over the years, then asked that all this be deducted from what were called improvements, but not real improvements they said. To their way of thinking flat land was not an improvement on hills and trees, clubrooms and a stand were not improvements on houses and a meeting place. These arguments were not accepted and deductions were not made. But many of the Te Ope people that had quarrelled and become divided thought the claims were fair and were angry over the decision. They began to give their strong support to the land occupiers again, and at that time more and more people moved onto the land to stay. More than had ever stayed on the land before.

But the final thing that happened was that there was a change in the government of the country. Promises had been made by the new party.

Even so it was not a great victory for the Te Ope people because there had to be compromise after all. Some were dissatisfied and angry with what was put forward and there were many meetings at which voices were raised and angry. There were weeks of talking, and then people came to an agreement. Part of the land was kept by them but some was given in repayment for improvements, even though the people did not agree that there had been improvements.

But at last they were able to begin building their house on their own land, to make their gardens, plant their trees where Rupena's parents had planted theirs such a long time before. At last they had a place to put their feet, and it was their own place, their own ancestral place, after all the years and all the trouble.

Our mother Roimata made books for us and we had stories of our own, in our own school. And some of the books were about all the interesting things that happened at Te Ope. When we grew old enough we went to the place where the real story was. The real story kept growing and growing as the years went by.

PART TWO

13

Dollarman

There was in the meeting-house a wood quiet.

It was the quiet of trees that have been brought in out of the wind, whose new-shown limbs reach out, not to the sky but to the people. This is the quiet, still, otherness of trees found by the carver, the shaper, the maker.

It is a watching quiet because the new-limbed trees have been given eyes with which to see. It is a waiting quiet, the ever-patient waiting that wood has, a patience that has not changed since the other tree life. But this tree quiet is an outward quiet only, because within this otherness there is a sounding, a ringing, a beating, a flowing greater than the tree has ever known before.

And the quiet of the house is also the quiet of stalks and vines that no longer jangle at any touch of wind, or bird, or person passing, but which have been laced and bound into new patterns and have been now given new stories to tell. Stories that lace and bind the earthly matters to matters not of earth.

Outside and about the meeting-house there was an early stillness. There was no movement or sound except for that which came from the quiet sliding, sidling of the sea.

But back in the houses, and beyond on the slopes, there was activity. At the houses washing was already out on the lines, morning meals were over and the cleaning up had been done. The vacuum cleaners had been through. Steps had been swept and there was a smell of cooking – of mutton and chicken and fish, watercress and cabbage, bread and pies.

In the hills the saws that had sounded since early morning were now still. Branches had been trimmed from the felled scrub, and the wood stacked and bound. The horse waited, occasionally snorting, stamping, or swinging its tail, but not impatiently. Then the tied wood bundle was attached to the chains coming from the big collar. The horse was led down the scented track under the dark shelves of manuka. Tools were picked up by those who went ahead to make sure the path was clear, while others followed to watch and steady the load.

At the bottom of the hill the horse and workers emerged from the cool dark into the sharp edges of light. The wood was unhitched at the woodstack. The collar and hames and chains were taken from the horse and put in the shed.

Work was over for the day. The money man was coming, to ask again for the land, and to ask also that the meeting-house and the urupa be moved to another place.

There was in the meeting-house a warmth.

It was the warmth that wood has, but it was also the warmth of people gathered. It was the warmth of past gatherings, and of people that had come and gone, and who gathered now in the memory. It was the warmth of embrace, because the house is a parent, and there was warmth in under the parental backbone, enclosement amongst the patterned ribs. There was warmth and noise in the house as the people waited for Mr Dolman to speak, Dolman whom they had named 'Dollarman' under the breath. Because although he had been officially welcomed he was not in the heart welcome, or at least what he had to say was not.

'. . . so that's what it is, development, opportunity, just as I've outlined to you, by letter. First class accommodation, top restaurants, night club, recreation centre with its own golf links – eventually, covered parking facilities . . . and then of course the water amenities. These water amenities will be the best in the country and will attract people from all over the world . . . launch trips, fishing excursions, jet boating, every type of water and boating activity that is possible. Endless possibilities – I've mentioned the marine life areas . . . your shark tanks . . .'

(Plenty of sharks around . . .)

'. . . trained whales and seals etcetera. As I've outlined in

writing, and as Ive discussed with Mr um . . . here and
. . . one or two others. And these water activities, the marine
life areas in particular, this is where you get off-season
patronage, where we get our families, our school parties at
reduced rates. So you see it's not just a tourist thing. It's an
amenity . . .'

(An amenity now . . . already . . .)

'. . . a much-needed amenity. Well there's this great potential you see, and this million-dollar view to be capitalised on.
And I'll mention once again that once we have good access,
it's all on, we can get into it. And benefit . . . not only ourselves but everyone, all of you as well. We'll be providing
top-level facilities, tourist facilities and so upgrade the industry
in this whole region. It'll boom. . . .'

'It's good that you have come here to meet us, meet all of
us, to discuss what you . . . your company has put forward.
Much of this you have outlined in your letters which we have
all read and talked about amongst ourselves. We have replied
to your letters explaining our feelings on what you have outlined and we have asked you to come here for a discussion.
Now you are here which is a good thing. We can meet face
to face on it, eyeball one another, and we can give our
thoughts and feelings and explanations more fully. As I say
we have all discussed this and I have been asked to speak on
behalf of all of us.

'This land we are on now – Block J136, the attached blocks
where the houses are, and J480 to 489 at the back of the
houses, is all ancestral land – the ancestral land of the people
here. And there are others too who don't live here now, but
this is still home to them. And a lot of them are here today,
come home for this meeting.

'Behind us are the hills. That was all once part of it too.
Well the hills have gone. A deal went through at a time when
people were too poor to hang on. It is something that is
regretted.

'But it won't happen . . . to the rest . . . what's left here.
Not even in these days of no work. We're working the land.
We need what we've got. We will not sell land, nor will access
be given. Apart from that, apart from telling you that none

of this land here will go, we have to tell you that none of us wants to see any of the things you have outlined. We've talked about it and there's no one, not one of us here, that would give an okay on it. None of those things would be of any advantage to our people here, in fact we know they would be greatly to our disadvantage. . . .'

'Well now, you've said that the developments here would be of no advantage to you. I'd like to remind you of what I've already said earlier. It's all job-creative. It'll mean work, well-paid work, right on your doorstep, so to speak. And for the area . . . it'll bring people . . . progress. . . .'

'But you see, we already have jobs, we've got progress. . . .'

'I understand, perhaps I'm wrong, that you're mostly unemployed?'

'Everything we need is here. This is where our work is.'

'And progress? Well it's not . . . obvious.'

'Not to you. Not in your eyes. But what we're doing is important. To us. To us that's progress.'

'Well maybe our ideas are different. Even so you wouldn't want to stand in the way. . . .'

'If we could. That's putting it straight. If we could stand in the way we would. But . . . as we've said, the hills have gone, your company, we believe, now being the owner. We can only repeat what we've said by letter. If you go ahead, which I suppose we can't prevent, then it won't be through the front. Not through here.'

'I'll explain about that, about access from behind. Access from behind is . . . not impossible, but almost. Certainly not desirable. We need to get people in, quick. . . .'

(Dollarman)

'. . . from all parts of the world. Mostly on arranged tours. Every detail taken care of. And need to be able to get them in, get them accommodated, comfortable . . .'

(Minus the dollar)

'. . . and they . . . people don't want to be travelling all those extra miles. Costly for them, costly for us. Then when they leave . . . of course we want to be able to move them . . . as conveniently as possible. But apart from all that, and even more important as far as smooth running goes, is

90

services, and workers. This is the main area of concern, why we have to get in and out quickly. It's costly, for people getting to work, for the trucks and vehicles coming in every day. There'd have to be miles of new road. And apart from costs there's time. But with good access, with your say-so we could be into it, in part, next season. . . .'

'Well as we've said, these ideas are not welcome to us people here. We can't stop you from setting up . . . what you've outlined, on what is now your land. But, I have to say very strongly, on behalf of us all here – we'll never let this house be moved. Never. Even if we could allow that, then there is the piece of land behind here where our dead are buried, which you would need also. That is a sacred site, as we've said in our letters. Our dead lie there. You will never get anyone to agree to it. No words. . . .'

'I hope I've made it clear. There would be no damage. Your hall . . .'

'Whare tipuna. Ancestral house. . . .'

'. . . would be put on trucks, transported, no cost to you. Set down exactly as it is now. No damage whatever. Two days from start to finish. And your cemetery. There's no real worry, let me assure you. Well it's nothing new, it's been done often enough before. A new site, somewhere nearby. And we've already had a think about this. All laid out, properly lawned, fenced, everything taken care of, everything in place . . .'

(Toe bone connected to your jaw bone . . .)

'. . . and you'll be well paid . . .'

(And there's the worry of it all)

'. . . for your land.'

'Mr Dolman, no amount of money. . . .'

'Well now wait a minute. We have, since our previous communication, had another look at the figures. I'd like to. . . .'

'Mr Dolman, I know we're hurrying you, but it's only fair that you should know. There is nothing you can say, no words, no amount of money. . . .'

'But look. I'm not sure that you have fully understood, and this is something I haven't pointed out previously. Your land here would skyrocket. Your value would go right up. . . .'

(Dollarman. There's the worry of it all . . .)

'You would have work, plus this prime amenity. On your doorstep, so to speak. . . .'

'We already have. . . .'

'Work. . . .'

'On our doorsteps. . . .'

'And a prime amenity which is land. . . .'

'Prime amenities of land and sea and people, as well as. . . .'

'A million dollar view, so to speak, that. . . .'

'Costs nothing.'

'Everything we want and need is here.'

'Well yes, yes of course. It's a great little spot. But maybe you have not seen its full potential. I'm not talking just about tourists now. I mentioned before the family people. I'm talking about giving families, school children, an opportunity to view our sea life. . . .'

'The dolphins come every second summer. . . .'

'Maybe so, but not for everyone, and not close, where people can see. . . .'

'Close enough to be believed.'

'I mean this way the public would have constant access. Our animals could be viewed any time. There would be public performances. . . .'

'Every second summer is public enough. . . .'

'And the seals. . . .'

'One comes now and again, then goes. . . .'

'Killer whales. You'd be denying people. . . .'

'The chance to watch you lay your head between its jaws. For money. . . .'

'Denying people this access, this facility.'

'We've never stopped people coming here, never kept anyone out. . . .'

'Denying families, and school children, their pleasures.'

'We've never told anyone to get off the beach or to stop catching fish. We've never stopped them cooking themselves in the sun, or prevented them from launching their boats. We've always allowed people to come here freely and we've often helped them out in bad weather. And, you know, these people – the families, the campers, the weekend fishing people – they'd back us up on this. They wouldn't like to see it all happen. They wouldn't like it.'

'We're not getting very far with this are we? I mean you invited me here and . . . I must say I expected you people to be more accommodating. . . .'

'Not so accommodating as to allow the removal of our wharenui, which is our meeting place, our identity, our security. Not so accommodating as to allow the displacement of the dead and the disruption of a sacred site.'

'I didn't expect people to be unreasonable. . . .'

'Unreasonable? Perhaps it is yourself that is being unreasonable if you think we would want pollution of the water out there, if you think we would want crowds of people, people that can afford caviare and who import salmon, coming here and using up the fish. . . .'

'And jobs. . . .'

'As we've told you, we have work. You want us to clean your toilets and dig your drains or empty your rubbish bins but we've got more important. . . .'

'I didn't say . . . And I wasn't . . . And you're looking back, looking back, all the time.'

'Wrong. We're looking to the future. If we sold out to you what would we be in the future?'

'You'd be well off. You could develop land, do anything you want.'

'I tell you if we sold to you we would be dust. Blowing in the wind.'

'Well I must say I find it difficult to talk sense. . . .'

(We notice . . .)

'One puff of the wind and that's it. And who is the first to point the finger then, when our people are seen to be broken and without hope? There's upset all round. . . .'

'Not so, not so. I mean I really believe that you people . . . have come a long way. . . .'

'Wrong again. We haven't come a long way at all. All we've done, many of us, is helped you, and people like you, get what you want. And we're all left out of it in the end. We've helped

93

build a country, all right. Worked in its factories, helped build its roads, helped educate its kids. We've looked after the sick, and we've helped the breweries and the motor firms to make their profits. We've helped export our crayfish and we've sent our songs and dances overseas. We've committed our crimes, done our good deeds, sat in Parliament, got educated, sung our hymns, scored our tries, fought in wars, splashed our money about. . . .'

'And you put all the blame. . . .'

'Blaming is a worthless exercise. That would really be looking back. It's now we're interested in. Now, and from now on.'

'Well then, that's what I mean. Why the concern with what's gone? It's all done with.'

'What we value doesn't change just because we look at ourselves and at the future. What we came from doesn't change. It's your jumping-off place that tells you where you'll land. The past is the future. If we ever had to move our tipuna it would be for our own reasons, some danger to the area, some act of God. It would not be for what you call progress, or for money. . . .'

'It's necessary in today's terms, money.'

'Nothing wrong with money as long as we remember it's food not God. You eat it, not worship it. . . .'

'Better too much than not enough, as they say.'

'Either way, too much or too little, you can become a slave.'

'Just as you can become a slave to past things. And to superstition . . . and all that . . . hoo-ha.'

'We have prepared a meal in the wharekai. You are welcome to eat before you go.'

'I'll go then. But I hope you'll all think about what we've discussed here today. There are ways. I'm a man who gets what he wants, and you should think about that. Have a look at the advantages to yourselves, to your children. I mean you've got something we require. We could work on a deal that would be satisfactory to all.'

'Something you require, yet you already have land, lots of land. . . .'

'We need this corner or the whole thing could fall through.'

'We give it to you and we fall through. We're slaves again, when we've only just begun to be free.'

14

Toko

I have my own story about when the Dollarman came. Our stories were changing. It is a story of a feeling and a knowing.

It is not the story of the Dollarman's first visit. He came back some months after his first visit, and he came back again and again bringing one person and then another, and each person he brought looked like a twin of himself and had a twin story to tell. The talk was always the same, and nothing became different because of their coming.

All of the people were proud of our Uncle Stan when the Dollarman came with all his money and his words, because he had words to match the Dollarman's words, and he had treasure enough to match the Dollarman's money.

Then one day the man came and said that work was to begin. They had had to minimise their plans, he said, because the access they had was not good access. Because of our lack of co-operation and foresight, he said, his company was being forced to cut down for the present. For the present, he said again. But one way or another, he said, he would persuade us to have sense, to have foresight, one way or another. One way or another, one way or another he kept saying, and that was when I had the feeling of fire. I had felt the strange seeds of it before when I was a child and my mother Roimata had held me close and felt afraid for me. But now I was not what you would call a child.

The fire began deep inside me and the redness of it went through me and leapt and scattered against the walls. The wood fathers and the wood mothers coloured and writhed, and their eyes were pinkish and flickering. There it was, and then it was gone. I was torched with the meaning of it all.

There was in the house a drawing in of breath, and a

sighing. There were sharp shouted words too, from my sister Tangimoana, though most of the people thought that this was not a right thing for her to do in the house of Rongo.

My father said that he was not sorry that the plans had been minimised, and wished that the man would leave the land for the people to enjoy as it was. 'It is an amenity as it is now, and always has been,' Hemi said.

Our Uncle Stan spoke about foresight. 'We have our eyes,' he said, 'We have our eyes, and after years of trying to please others we're going on our own, and we can see. There's no lack of foresight, as you put it. It's because we have foresight that we will not ever, not ever, let the land go. Take away the heart, the soul, and the body crumbles.'

But the man thought it was only words – words without thinking or meaning, words not chosen with care. 'We'll see,' the man said, 'We'll see about it.'

After that we had to send letters giving all our objections to the plans. These plans were not to do with the annexing of our land because our land could not be annexed. But they were to do with the excursions and watersports, the under-water zoo and the animal circus, the clapping seals, the man putting his head in the mouth of a whale, and all the things that had been planned. And when a letter came telling us how we could be involved, and how we could dress up and dance and sing twice a day and cook food in the ground, we wrote angrily in reply. Our singing and dancing was not for sale, we said, nor was our food cooked on stones. 'Let them put themselves out on the stones to cook,' I heard my uncle say, 'There will always be the cooled and soundproofed rooms for them to return to, from where they can look out over the water, silly as fantails and talking loud, but from where they do not hear the boat motors screaming. They won't hear the screaming,' he said, 'They've got no ears for the screaming.'

He said those things because he was angry and because he knew that the land and sea were an amenity already.

As we were 'objectors' there were other meetings to attend. We all went to where the meetings were held, all of us, to make the place full. We were not the only objectors because there were fishermen and weekend boat people, and environmentalists. Tangimoana brought some of her friends from university. They made a lot of noise too, which some of the family were not pleased about. So the chambers were full of people and noise, and the suit men were fanning themselves with envelopes and papers.

It was easy to understand why the suit men were in favour of the development because it would mean large numbers of summer visitors to the area, and that meant 'moving forward' if you could think of it that way. And even when it was not summer there would be good bargains for families and schools going to see the man's head in the mouth of a whale, and porpoises leaping two by two through burning circles and having smiling faces like high-wire-walking people and magic men. Smiling, smiling, but nothing to be known from their eyes.

And there would be profits for businesses, high rents, new transport companies, new eating places, golf and squash and saunas, and everything to interest the golden people.

But there were two different parts. There was one part where we were objectors because we were anxious about the land and sea. The hills and sea did not belong to us but we wished to see them kept clean and free. We could only be objectors along with others who liked to swim and camp and fish, and who did not want the sea or land changed. We, like them, did not want the company to make zoos and circuses in the sea, or to put noise and pollution there, or to line the shore with palaces and castles, and souvenir shops, or to have restaurants rotating above the sea, lit up at night like star crafts landing their invaders on the shore.

Because soon there would be no fish, only pet ones that you went in lit underground tunnels to see at shark-feeding time, or any time you wanted. If you paid.

Well we wanted the fish to be in the sea like ordinary fish, the stingrays to roam in the evenings as they always do. We wanted our eyes to know the place where they would meet the tide whether it was low or high.

My father Hemi said that the land and sea was our whole life, the means by which we survived and stayed together. 'Our whanau is the land and sea. Destroy the land and sea,

98

we destroy ourselves. We might as well crack open our heads, take the seed, and throw it on the flame.'

Then next there was our own land with our own carved house built by the people long before, and carved by a man who had given life and breath. This house of his, of ours, carried forward the stories of the people of long ago, but told about our lives today as well. There were crayfish, eels, moki and codfish all made into patterns in our house. There were karaka trees, pohutukawa, ngaio, nikau and kakaho, and patterns made from sea waves, rocks and hills, and sun, rain and stars. There were patterns made out of crying and knowledge and love and quarrelling. There was a pattern, or a person, for every piece of our lives. The house was polished and loved by my first mother Mary every day.

And behind the house is where the dead are buried. These were the places wanted by the money men, that they would pay thousands of dollars to have. These were the places that the council people tried to assist the money men to get from us. My mother Roimata said that they think differently in their heads and have different importances.

But we would not let them take our land, or move our house or our dead, no matter how often the gold man came with his anger and his different way of thinking in his head. My brother Manu was afraid of him and called out in sleep. My brother James was not afraid, and listened carefully so that he would know. My sister Tangi was not afraid of the man but she did have fear. I, like my sister, was not afraid of the man but did have fear because of a special knowing. I did not call out in sleep as my brother did, and I did not call out in anger as my sister did, but I had a special knowing that gave me fear.

One day when we were out in the gardens there came noise from far back in the hills. It was the road machines, making a way for development to begin, and it was the sound of dynamite blasting the hills away. But these roads were not the roads that the money men had wanted to make. The roads they wanted were roads in front of our houses, and through our wharenui and urupa. The roads had been shown to us on maps by the money men again and again, who had kept saying that our house could be shifted without cost to us. But when asked where it could be shifted to, they said that perhaps it could be shifted nearer to town, to a more central place.

Everybody had laughed then, because the man had not understood that the house was central already and could not be more central. The man had a surprised look when the people laughed and looked down at his clothing as though he could suddenly be dressed strangely. It was then that we all realised that the man had not, had never, understood anything we had ever said, and never would.

My uncle tried to explain it all again. I think he felt sorry for the man. My sister Tangimoana was not sorry for the man at all. She called him a stupid bastard.

Now there was a very strange thing. I was sitting up close by my Granny Tamihana. We had the mattresses down so that we could be comfortably seated, and our rugs were spread on the mattresses. We did not get in under our rugs because the weather was warm.

Earlier when preparing the house for the meeting some had thought that we should bring in a table for the man's plans and papers, and a chair for the man to sit on, but my mother Roimata disagreed.

She said to let the man be like everyone else because that would be good psychology.

'You mean let him sit on the floor in his suit and his sock feet so he'll feel a fool, him not being used to our ways?' Tangimoana said.

'Tangi I didn't mean that, not exactly. I meant let the boot be on the other foot for a change. Let him feel what we sometimes feel . . . in different situations.'

'It's exactly what you meant no matter how nice you put it,' said Tangimoana. And all the women laughed while they unrolled the whariki and the boys put the mattresses down on them.

When my cousins Paul and Stanny came with a table and a chair for the man the aunties sent them away again saying the table and chair were not needed.

And when Tangi called out 'stupid bastard' to the man, my father Hemi and my Uncle Stan, who were seated by where the man was standing talking to us, frowned and were angry with her but they didn't look up. The man kept talking and his face was red and furious.

It was so strange. My father and uncle were frowning and upset, and the money man was angry and red, and then my old Granny began to shake. I was close by her. I turned my head to look at her. Her forehead was resting on her skinny hand, which was like a chook hand, or really a foot of a chook, and she was laughing and laughing.

At first I didn't understand, with all the angriness of the man and the annoyed manner of the other older people, why my Granny was shaking like an earthquake and hiding her face with her hand. Then my mother Roimata on the other side of Granny put her head down too, and her shoulders were lumping up and down. Mary, who was sitting on the other side of me reached over and began to tickle my chin. She had forgotten all about the man standing there, red in his sock feet. Her remembering is not good in some things. I began to laugh too.

There was beginning to be noise and a murmur in the house, the way there often is when you have finished with something and had enough.

It was enough right then. The man began to collect his papers together. My father thanked him and then we stood to sing the hymn which would conclude our meeting. But I did not stand because my family did not wish it. It was not easy for me to stand. My Granny remained seated with me and so did my first mother, Mary.

As the hymn ended everyone moved out of the house, the children to play with their ball out on the marae, and the adults towards the wharekai.

The man was standing with my father. Hemi, I knew, would be asking the man to stay and have lunch with all of us in the wharekai, but the man was shaking his head.

There we were with everyone else gone. My father and the man were going towards the door. My mother Mary was standing on her mattress singing to the house, to the shadowy, quick-eyed figures, rocking her body from side to side and beginning to sing louder and louder. My Granny stood and reached my sticks to me. She waited for me, bent and old, wiping her laughing tears.

I pulled myself up on my sticks. At the same time I looked up, and my eyes met the man's eyes as he looked back. Eyes angry, but as well as anger there was something else coming into his eyes that came from the anger, but anger was only part of it.

Right then I saw what the man saw as he turned and looked at the three of us and as my eyes met his eyes. I saw what he saw. What he saw was brokenness, a broken race. He saw in my Granny, my Mary and me, a whole people, decrepit, deranged, deformed. That was what I knew. That was when I understood, not only the thoughts of the man, but also I understood the years of hurt, sorrow and enslavement that fisted within my Granny Tamihana's heart. I understood, all at once, all the pain that she held inside her small and gentle self.

And the pain belonged to all of us, I understood that too. I understood that my sister's angry words shouted in the house of wood, the house of stories, the house of tipuna – shouted into the domain of Rongo which is the domain of peace – were a relief and a release for my Granny, causing her to shake and laugh herself to tears.

I was the only one who saw the carved hate and anger on the face of the man as he stepped into the afternoon, out into the shouting of kids scrambling after their ball on the marae.

15

Roimata

Everything we need is here, Hemi said. It's true, and he's always known it. What Toko said was also true – the stories had changed.

Once we went back to the land there were not enough hours in the day for what needed to be done, and every day our work continued until after dark. With the help of a horse, and later a small tractor and truck, the land was broken in. Seaweed and other manures were spread in the winter months and turned under. Trenches were made for compost. A good market was found for potatoes and pumpkins for the first year's harvest, and each year after that the gardens were added to, new crops were tried, and the market slowly widened. But before the market we had ourselves to provide for. Our homes were full as more of the whanau returned because of jobs becoming more and more scarce, and as accommodation became more difficult to find and to afford.

There was work for everyone here, even though it was not the paid work that most had been accustomed to. Some were pleased and relieved to be back. Others were here more reluctantly, and did not stay long. Ours was a chosen poverty, though 'poverty' was not a good word for it.

The stories were of existence, of survival, of being up before light, breakfasting on reheated vegetables, bread and tea. Then by first light, those who worked in the gardens would be out stooping into the soil.

Our two youngest ones were not little children any more. They did not need me so much for their schooling because they had discovered how to learn for themselves. They themselves knew what it was they wanted to learn, and why. They knew how to go about getting the knowledge that they wanted. But Manu and Toko and I kept a corner of the wharekai free, where the little children of the whanau came to talk and sing and read and write each morning. We had time enough for that. We could not afford books so we made our own. In this way we were able to find ourselves in books. It is rare for us to find ourselves in books, but in our own books we were able to find and define our lives.

But our main book was the wharenui which is itself a story, a history, a gallery, a study, a design structure and a taonga. And we are part of that book along with family past and family yet to come.

The land and the sea and the shores are a book too, and we found ourselves there. They were our science and our sustenance. And they are our own universe about which there are stories of great deeds and relationships and magic and imaginings, love and terror, heroes, heroines, villains and fools. Enough for a lifetime of telling. We found our own universe to be as large and as extensive as any other universe that there is.

For our stories there were not enough hours in each day, but we spent a part of each morning with the little ones of the whanau while their parents worked. Toko, who had had by then to slow his movements down, spent more and more time with the children, and with those who worked in the kitchen. His brother was always nearby to walk with him or to bring him to the gardens when he wanted to come.

It was easy enough to laugh at the state of our clothing. Some of the skirts and jeans had been mended so many times that they were almost made up of patches. The socks and jerseys had been darned so many times that we could call them new again. Many went barefoot for most of the year to save their shoes for the cold months.

Our homes needed painting but there was no money for paint. Some of the fences needed nailing but there was no time for it until winter came. Our cars had been sold because there was no money for repairs, and no money for petrol. But we had the truck and tractor, there was money enough for that.

Some of us still had television, but once a set broke down there was no money to fix it. And there was no time any more

104

for watching television, and not much liking for it because it did not define us. There was little indication through television that we existed at all in our own land. There was little on television that we could take to our hearts.

There was money enough to pay for electricity, rates and petrol for the machines. There was enough for tea, flour, soap and cigarettes, but little more than that. Hemi's brother Stan sometimes said, 'The gardens are great, the people are pohara,' but it was only said so that we could laugh at ourselves. We were not pohara. Our family had known greater hardship than this in the past, and had known greater poverty. Some had survived, become whole again, others had never mended.

We were not pohara. Our chosen hardship was something that was good and uplifting to all of us, a biting on the pebble that keeps an edge on the teeth. But we did not know how events were to turn and all but destroy the spirit that gave life and energy and strength to all of us.

We were not pohara. We were whole and life was good. The gardens would soon be in full production and perhaps then we would have warm shoes, perhaps then we would have meat on our plates. If we could not it did not matter.

We would not have wished that the old lady in her ninety-third year would be in the wharekai daily, sitting by the fireplace preparing vegetables, but it was what she chose to do. 'I'll help my Mary,' she said. 'You leave us two here and not to worry. Otherwise I rattle in my own kitchen good for nothing. Go to your other work.'

We would not have wanted to take Mary away from the work she loved, and we did not. Mary would spend the mornings in the wharekai with Granny Tamihana preparing food, washing teatowels and tablecloths, mopping floors and washing down table-tops. In the afternoons, Mary would as usual go on her own to the wharenui to dust and polish, to converse with the tipuna, and to sing in the house of the people.

James was not with us all the time. He was with the koroua who taught him to carve, regaining a skill for the whanau. They were sometimes at Te Ope and sometimes elsewhere, depending on where they were needed. But James returned to us and to the gardens in the busy seasons, even though we had told him it was not necessary for him to do so.

Tangimoana was at university because the whanau had asked her to go there and study law. There was enough money for that. She returned in the holidays and divided her time between sleeping, and working in the wharekai or gardens. But also she had study and assignments to do.

The man did not come back again after the last time when he left in anger. No one came and we heard no more for over a year. We were busy with our work and had almost put the development proposals out of mind when a letter arrived. The company was to go ahead with its plans but would have to go ahead without the use of the land on which our urupa and wharenui stood, unless at that late stage we would reconsider. Also they asked for permission for the construction company to use our private access while development took place.

We did not reconsider, and did not give permission for the use of our road. In this we were supported by other people who, over the years, had become friends. They were fishermen and family people who had always used our road and the beach in a family way. They were people who did not want to see development in the area, and did not want the destruction of trees and the flattening of hills, and did not want to have the road used by big trucks and land-working machines.

After the letter we heard nothing more for some weeks. No one came. Then one day when we were out in the gardens detonations sounded as from far away, and later that day the sound of road machines was carried to us by the northerly. It was the construction company building access through the back way. We turned back to the gardens because there was nothing else we could do.

Every day the sounds came closer until one day we could see the yellow cuttings that the yellow machines had made, and the yellow clothes and the yellow hard hats that the men wore who worked the yellow machines. There was nothing we could do, or that's what we thought, because that part of the land had gone from us long before.

There were others who did not think as we did, that nothing could be done. Their letters, objections and actions were widely reported and discussed, but we turned away. We were busy with our gardens and our nets, and busy learning all that could be learned about the land and the sea. We were busy telling and retelling the stories and histories of a people and a place, and learning or relearning a language which was our own, so that we could truly call it our own again. We worked for our own survival and we tried not to look towards the hills, tried not to hear the sounds that came from there.

Then one morning a small group of people came by our place and said that they were going up to sit on the new road, and that they were not going to allow the road construction to go any further. They were going to sit in front of the bull-dozers they said, and they asked us to join them. We looked up and saw that others were already there, waiting on the road. We did not join them. It did not seem right to us, to sit on land that no longer belonged to us.

The roadmen laughed when they arrived at work and found the group of people with their placards and signs. They did not start up their machines but went away and boiled the billies and played cards until the bosses came. That's what the people told us later.

The bosses shouted and raved and so did the people, but the people did not move until the police came. Some of them went home when the police came, but some were arrested and taken away in vans. We could hear them shouting about the road and the destruction of the land. It was afternoon before work on the road began again.

The next morning some of the young ones from here went to join the group that had reformed up on the road, though not everyone in the whanau approved of them doing this. They hurried home when the police came, being careful to avoid arrest.

'Some of them are our own relations,' James said, 'Driving the big machines.' He said two names. 'They said they didn't want to give up their jobs because their jobs would only be given to others and the road will be made anyway.'

'Of course they shouldn't give up their jobs,' said Hemi.

'All this is no fault of theirs, nothing to do with them. A man and his family have to eat.'

'They spoke to us,' James said, 'Asked us if we lived here, and said who they were, they're Rihanas.'

Hemi and I both knew who they were.

'There was trouble,' Hemi said.

'Been inside, both of them,' said James. 'And not easy for them to get work.'

'Go up there tomorrow and bring them home,' Hemi said. 'Their grandfather was from here and their parents brought them here when they were children. After that they went to Aussie to live. Go up there tomorrow and bring them home.'

That was when we met, or met again, Matiu and Timoti.

The barricades and protests lasted just a week. There was nothing anyone could do.

But it was soon after that that letters began to arrive again. We were offered more and more money for the land on which our wharenui and our urupa stood, land which would give good access to the developd sites, and allow greater development. We were promised too that our own roadway which gave access to our homes, and which we had built and which we maintained ourselves, would be upgraded. The developers would widen and seal the road as well as kerb, channel and light it – if they could also use it. But we did not wish to help them in the things they wanted to do so we did not give permission for our road to be used, even though the road, as it was, was expensive and difficult for us to maintain. It was rutted and pot-holed, and flooded sometimes in winter.

The developers were angry at our constant refusals but that was because they did not understand that our choice was between poverty and self-destruction. Yet poverty is not a good word. Poverty is destructive too. We did not have real poverty. We had homes and enough good food, or nearly always enough. We had people and land and a good spirit, and work that was important to us all.

One evening after karakia Stan read to us the most recent letter telling the sum the developers were offering for the land.

We were shocked by the figure read out to us. The amount of money offered told us that the developers were desperate for our piece of land, and this desperation was frightening to us. It caused us to wonder what could happen, what they would do, once they had accepted that we could not be bought. We wondered if their power and money could be used in a different way. It was worrying to realise the desperation that was behind the offer of such a large sum.

In the meantime trucks were bringing materials in. The big machines were clearing large areas of land. The hills were being sliced away, and rock and rubble was being pushed into the sea.

It was spring then, and the gardens, the big gardens, were soft and tender and green.

16

Roimata

So we tried to turn our backs on the hills and not look up. The hills did not belong to us any more. At the same time we could not help but remember that land does not belong to people, but that people belong to the land. We could not forget that it was land who, in the beginning, held the secret, who contained our very beginnings within herself. It was land that held the seed and who kept the root hidden for a time when it would be needed. We turned our eyes away from what was happening to the hills and looked to the soil and to the sea.

That summer of the rain the earth had plenty to give, as did the sea.

It is not important to have meat on the plate when you are a shore-dweller. If you are a shore-dweller there are always sea gleanings to go with the root.

At any time of the year, and in any weather, we could get paua and kina when the tide was low. On any calm day we could set the nets for butterfish, moki, shark or kahawai, although the catch was not always good. Occasionally we would pull in a snapper or a conger eel on a handline thrown from shore. If the bigger fish were not around then we could get small cod from the rocks or kelpie from the weed-beds.

We tried not to look at the hills and we tried to ignore, just adjacent to us, the changing shoreline, and tried not to talk about the yellow mud colour of the sea.

That summer of the rain I was the one who usually went with Hemi to collect the nets in the early evening, while the younger ones were busy with other work. I love very much the free feeling of pulling out over the water in the dinghy, and the brisk salt smell of the sea.

At that time we were setting the nets at one of the furthermost netting places because of the mud that now coloured the more shoreward fishing spots. In this place we were still able to see the nets below the surface, and on windless days we could look down and see the catch, if there was one, gleaming along the net line.

On the night that the rain began Hemi and I went out late to pick up the nets. It was a busy time because we had been packing and loading the first crops for the markets. The wind was coming up so we did not want to leave the nets overnight as we sometimes did.

Some of the children, who had already had their evening meal at the wharekai, were down on the beach piling driftwood for a fire. Most of the light had gone, and the white summered sticks that they collected were pale, bonelike, in the part-dark. The children helped us carry the dinghy down to the water.

I took up the oars while Hemi walked the boat out a short distance before stepping in over the stern. He steadied himself then moved the net crates into position.

Even after a day of heavy work there is strength to pull a small boat out over the sea. There is joy in it. I pulled fast and hard until I was breathless, and then Hemi took over from me. The wind was slight, causing some movement on the surface of the water as I leaned over to take hold of the first net buoy. The boat spun as I grasped it and a spray of water spilled onto me, wetting face, hair and clothes, stinging and cold, but there was joy in that too after the hot, hard work of the gardens. The rain that threatened had not yet begun.

I took the oars again to steady the boat while Hemi pulled the first net in. There was only one fish in the first net and that was a small snapper. 'Hardly worth the ducking,' I heard Hemi say. I swung the boat round and pulled a few strokes to where the second net was. It was dark by then.

Back on shore was the glow of the fire that the children

111

had lit, and where they now waited to see what the catch would be.

To the right of them the lights of the wharekai were on. Through the light, people, as shadows, moved to and fro. In the darkness the hills, the broken hills, had become whole again.

We were close to the second buoy before we saw it. The water had roughened and I had to turn the dinghy several times before Hemi could grasp the ball and rope. 'Heavy,' he said as he began to pull in. 'Kahawai,' I heard him say, and I could see the soft shine of them, one for every metre of net that he drew in over the stern. 'Worth the ducking after all,' he said. He hauled in the end buoy and lifted it into the basket. We were both wet by then as small waves slapped the boat's sides and splashed up and in. 'Worth a wet arse, well worth.' Hemi took the oars from me to hurry us to shore.

The children waiting on the beach would not have seen us in the dark, but they would have listened for, and heard, the creaking, the dip and splash sounds of the oars. As we came close they piled the wood onto the fire so that there would be light for us to come in by, enough light to enable them to see the catch of fish, and light for us to clean the fish by.

Some of the older children were there to help carry the boat up, and they had brought knives with them, or found shells so that they could help with the scaling and cleaning.

There was surprise about the snapper because they were rare in the bay. It was not often that we netted one, although there were other places further round where we knew we could get them. To go snapper fishing plans had to be made, the weather needed to be settled, and a day needed to be set aside. But at that time there were no spare days that could be given to line fishing, or to going to deeper grounds, so it was not often we had the tamure to eat.

I cannot say that any of us missed it from our plates even though, generally, it is a much sought-after fish, a fish which takes the bait strongly and comes heavy on the line. The tamure has flesh that is pale and succulent. It does not bleed. The head of the tamure is a celebration, but the tamure is

112

not a feast. It is not the life of the shore-dweller, is not the sustainer of the netters of fish whose wellbeing depends on what the nets will yield. Or at least in these parts it is not.

Here, it is a fish for those who fish at leisure, who have motors heavy enough to get them quickly to the grounds and quickly home when there is a wind change.

The kahawai though is life, or to us it is. It is a fish for the shore-liver whether it is netted or taken on the spinner. It is not necessary to have meat on the plate when there is kahawai. Here we have a closeness to it – to its leaping beauty, to its dark bleeding flesh. It has a greenstone silverness about it and its eye is small and gaudy, like the paua-shell eyes that watch unblinking round all the many edges of the night.

Hands took the bow as the dinghy rode in, hands steadied it as we stepped out. Hands lifted the net baskets out, lifted and carried the dinghy up to the high ground.

I stood by the fire to warm and dry myself while the nets were unravelled and the fish taken from them to be gutted and scaled. Perhaps the rain had begun earlier, but we had not noticed it while out on the sea. There were small drops, intermittent, not enough to affect the good fire that was warming me and drying out the wet clothing.

They worked swiftly at cleaning the fish, knowing that the rain would soon be heavy, but also because we were looking forward to the evening meal which would be waiting for us in the wharekai. It was good to feel hunger and to know there was food. It was good to know that there was food for the next day. It was good to be cold and to know it would be warm in the wharekai.

And then it was done. The children began to pick up the kahawai, wanting to be the ones to carry them, high-pitched and eager.

'Carry them. . . .'
'Carry. . . .'
'I can, I. . . .'
'I want, I can. . . .'
'Me. . . .'

113

Children bending, slipping hands into the gills of the kahawai, straightening, and standing for a moment in the fire's light, faces shadowed, blood running down their arms. The kahawai is heavy in flesh and how it bleeds. They bleed. The children ran towards the wharekai with the kahawai. Bleeding. The rain was beginning to fall heavily.

'They bleed, how our children bleed. . . .'

The wharekai let us in. There was joy at the catch, and at the smell of hot food.

'They do, and we don't forget, but . . . there's food for tomorrow.'

It was still raining when we woke next morning, and steady rain fell for most of the day.

We spent the day doing indoor work that there had been little time for. We prepared vegetables for the freezer, mended clothes, tidied sheds and sorted equipment, and painted some cupboards and ledges in the wharekai. The rain, after all the dry days we'd been having, was a relief. There had never been cause in the past for anyone to be worried by a day, or two days, or a week of rain, except that the road could become muddy and impassable.

That evening lightning panned through the wharekai, and thunder sounded. Rain kept up its heavy beating. But there was warmth in the steady sound of it as the big dishes of fish pie were carried to the tables.

The following morning we woke to water, surrounding our houses and entering some of them, and water spread like a lake where the gardens had been. We discovered later in the morning that one side of the urupa had begun to slide away. The rain had stopped by then and there was no sound at all.

114

17

Toko

The stories changed. There is a story of water, but there is also a story of colours, and a story of stars.

In the water story the gardens were ruined by rain and mud, and one side of the urupa began to slide. The sea became silted and yellow, the colour of the broken hills. The creek went in ways that it had never gone before. It was a world not thought of but only imagined.

It was like looking out on the long-ago time when the goddess, in anger, had set the world on fire to punish her descendant for his tricks. And the uri was afraid and had to call out to hard and lasting rain to save him and save the earth. It was like looking out on that long-ago, drenched-earth time. Between them, the goddess and the uri had been able to give fire as a gift, a taonga for the people. But, if what happened to our land in the time of rain was like what happened in the long-ago time, what was the wrong that was being punished? Was there a taonga that would be gifted as a result? Was there some good that would come from what was not good?

There had been heavier rain in other years, and more long-lasting rain. No harm had ever come of it, except that our road along the front had often become ridged and guttered, and was sometimes in bad condition for most of the winter. The road was our only worry when there had been heavy rain.

And it was a silent world when we woke. The rain had stopped. There was no wind. There was no sound of water, not even from the sea, only the sight of water trapped over the land. On the side of the little hill of the urupa there was a bare patch showing rock. Our eyes turned there, fearing the sudden white sight of bone.

All of this happened because of the stripping of the hills,

the cutting away of the land, the dislodgement of the sea rock and the blocking of the shore, or that's what we thought. But these were not the only reasons, as we later found.

There was stillness. There was no sound except for the wailing of women that swells and recedes the way the sea does, the way the wind does, the way the heart does at certain times.

We made our way through the water to the beach, then walked along the shore to the meeting-house. We had our karakia there, then the younger men went to get the dinghies while others waded to the sheds for shovels and ropes. The gear was put into the dinghies and those who were able began to make their way towards the back of the land, round the base of the hills, moving along beside the usual route of the creek, but the creek was going in ways it had never gone before. I would have been pleased to have gone with them, but there were many things by then that I could not do. I was helped over to the wharekai where Mary, Tangimoana, my aunties and I waited with the children.

At the back of the land where the creek runs round the base of the hills the people found the rock and chunks of concrete and bitumen that had been piled in the creek bed, but even seeing it they did not think at first of anything that would have been deliberately done. They were angry about the lack of care of the road builders but did not think of intention. It took them half of the day to clear the blockage. By then much of the water had soaked into the land.

It was while the people were away clearing the creek that we saw some men come down off the hills. The water had gone down a little by then, but they had to wade still. They walked about where the gardens had been, and then went on towards the urupa, and then we lost sight of them for a while. Later we saw them coming towards the wharekai. It was Matiu and Timoti with three others.

They were wet and muddy and would not come inside.

'Where's Uncle?' It was anger that caused Matiu to shout through the doorway.

'Up the back,' I said. 'They went early, without breakfast, and haven't come home yet.'

No one knew why it was that Matiu was shouting into the wharekai, or why Timoti was crying, or why their three mates looked at the ground and would not look up. They turned to go.

'If you're going, could you . . . take food?' my aunty asked them. They turned back and sat down on the step to wait, then Timoti said, shouting, 'Aunty someone done this to you, to all of us. Someone from the job.'

'It's the cutting away of the hills,' said Aunty. 'The clearing.'

'Someone done it. We've just seen. . . .'

And Tangimoana said, 'Why? What do you mean?'

'Channelling down the side. . . .'

'Rain,' Aunty said. 'And the clearing.'

'No, someone. Cleared a place and . . . channelled the water to run down, to where the urupa . . . And the urupa starting to wash away.'

Aunty did not speak for several moments. No one spoke. Then she said, 'If it's right . . . if people did, but I don't think. . . .'

'Who? Who from the job?' Tangimoana was shouting too.

'Someone. Don't know who, but we know they're a crook lot, they're dealers. We're packing it in, that's the finish for us . . . We'll take the kai up and see what's doing up back.'

They turned to go, then Matiu stopped and said, 'It was yesterday, rained off yesterday, no work. But someone was here . . . in the rain, doing . . . this mess.'

'Well, if it's right,' Aunty said.

'And there might be more too, up the creek. Because Uncle and them . . . What's taking them so long? But it wouldn't be workers that done it, it'll be bosses. . . .'

'And no fault of yours, if it's right. If it's right,' Aunty kept saying.

Because it was difficult to believe, or at least it was difficult to believe for some people, but not for me. I was the one who had seen the rage and hate on the man's face when he was there last. My singing mother Mary had been with me but

117

she does not see rage and hate. My Granny was there, but she is old and bent, and was stooping, passing my sticks to me. It was only I, along with the watching house, who saw the hardened face, who watched a man stride unseeing into light, unhearing into the shouting afternoon. Even so, rage and hatred are not easily understood. It is not easy for those who do not have power, to understand the force of power.

There were other people around by then, in boots and coats. Some were reporters, making a way to the hillside from where they could look down. There was a man with a camera standing nearby, moving from one foot to another as Matiu and Timoti started out. The man was not dressed for water.

'I'll follow you,' Tangimoana was saying to Matiu and Timoti. 'With the hot drink, in a sec.'

Can he speak to the chief?

'Is there anyone in particular you would like to see?' Tangimoana asked.

'The chief,' he said.

'Perhaps I can help you?'

'Well who's in charge?'

'Of what?' Her replies were becoming shorter.

'Of. . . . Of. Well I haven't got much time. And if I could go straight to the top?'

'What of? A tree?'

'Look, I just want to know who's in charge here so I can get permission. I want some photos, and I need some people. . . .'

'This is where we live. We're all in charge.'

'But you've got a chief. Or someone, you know, who has the say, looks after things.'

'We all have the say, all of us together, all look after things.'

'I um . . . well that's a bit unusual isn't it?'

'No.'

'Well I mean . . . look all I want is a few photos. And I could just go and take them, but I actually need a few people, for the shots. If a few could get out, you know, where the water is . . . before it all goes down.'

'Sorry. Too busy.'

'Only a few minutes.'

'No.'

'Well look I'll speak to . . . someone else . . . in authority.'

'Find someone then. Or just go out there and take your photos like everyone else seems to be doing. You don't need us out there shamming things up for you.'

'Well I've got a tight schedule and. . . .'

'Haven't we all? Come on Tania, we'll get going with this.'

The photographer put his head in the door and said, 'Where's the chief?'

'Will I do?' Aunty Rina asked.

'I was hoping for a few people, to just . . . come over the way there, for a few shots.'

'Go ahead,' she said. 'Have a look. Might be someone around out there. Can you do something for us Toko?' she said to me. 'Phone up Hoani. Tell him if he can come out to the urupa. We've got to have a karakia up there. Tell him urgent. And tell him bring some boots, or tell him might be we can find some for him here.'

The man with the camera went then, and stood for a while by the roadside, but he was not dressed for water and mud. He made his way along to the road where his car was parked. I went to phone the priest.

It was about two hours later that one of the children who had been up the hill looking out came back and said the people were returning. The water had gone down a lot by then, so we, with Hoani, prepared to go out towards the urupa to meet them.

'I'll walk,' I said.

'It's a long way.' For me.

'And too muddy for the chair.'

But my brother was already helping me remove the heavy shoes.

'Leave your sticks, leave your shoes,' he said. 'Too hoha, come on, Puti.'

He and our cousin shouldered in under my armpits and linked hands behind me, as I draped my arms about their necks.

119

'Go on ahead, we'll catch you shortly,' our Aunty said. 'What about you, Kui? We need you there with Hoani.'

'All of us,' said Granny Tamihana. 'All the kids, babies, all the whanau, everyone.'

There were people about, some writing in notebooks, others taking photos. Some had come to look, and others to help. Some were friends – those who had tried to stop the road from being made and who had been angry at the cutting of the hills, the destruction of trees, the disturbance of rocks of the hills and shore.

'It's because of that,' they said.

'It could be more than that,' Aunty Rina said.

'We've come to help, maybe clean up. Whatever.'

'Come with us,' our Aunty said. 'We're going to have karakia, a service, up at the urupa . . . our cemetery. Started to wash away, you see. We don't know what we'll find, what needs doing, but . . . we need help, with the old lady, the kids.'

She turned to speak to her daughter.

'Get some gumboots for Granny, Babe, and a warm jacket for her, and for you too. You too Mary, you get your boots and coat. Come on kids, boots on, do your jackets up.'

So the people who had become our friends came with us through the mud carrying the children. They stood with us as we met up with the others and as we began to tangi for all that had happened, and for family long gone and recently gone, but who were amongst us still. We all stood close together about the urupa as we chanted the karakia and sang the waiata tangi. It was our urupa, where as younger children we had listened and played, where we had told our stories and said our dreams into the ground.

18

The urupa

Granny Tamihana always gave them the first flowers of each season to take up to the graves. In one season there were red and gold gladioli, scarlet geraniums, and hydrangeas that were rust and mauve. In another there were dahlias and snap-dragons that were white and purple and wine, and there were leafy branches of kotukutuku with dark hanging bells. In another there were rust and amber wallflowers and heavy brown chrysanthemums. Then there were the snowdrops, freesias, jonquils, daffodils, and handfuls of green.

She would give them the special water containers that she kept under the shed and instructions on what was allowed and what was not allowed, and instructions on what needed to be done.

The children always filled the containers at the creek before starting up the small hill to the urupa. On the way up there was a large manuka that stood by itself, that they should not touch, so they did not touch it. They would move on to the narrow path that led to the gate, helping each other, helping Toko so that he would not lose balance and fall.

Once inside the fence they would sit down to rest, then after a while begin to walk about, keeping to the narrow paths, being careful not to step on the places. They would read the stones and discuss the dead, retelling the stories they'd heard and told over and over again.

Manu said that Uncle Pere Thompson had been as big as a mountain, and that when he died people had had to take the roof off his house to get him out. It was worse than a horse dying inside, he said. But James didn't think there had been anything about a mountain. He reckoned that their uncle was just a fat man with a coffin the size of a kitchen that it took forty men to carry. The men had straps over their shoulders, the same straps that you have when you lift a piano, or maybe they used a crane, he said.

Then Tangimoana remembered that there really was something about a mountain because the diggers had taken hours and hours to dig the hole. The men had started digging early in the morning and the sun was hard on them before they finished, and it was nearly time for the burial. One of the digging men had collapsed and they thought he had died too, but it was because he had not had food or drink, and because they had all hurried to get the digging finished before burying time.

But the earth dug out from the deep hole had made a big pile, like a mountain, and when all the people had come to the burial they'd had to stand on the slopes of the mountain so that they could watch Uncle Pere go down.

Manu said that he knew Pere Thompson had been as big as a mountain, and Toko said but not always. Because when Uncle was young he had been as skinny as a handle, but when he was old he was very enormous. He used to make toffee for kids Toko said, but that was when Dad and Uncle Stan and mother Mary were kids. And he twisted the toffee into curly sticks. Nobody else could. His legs were like the pyramids of Egypt, he said.

Well Aunty Emma was married to a German spy. She pushed him off his bike one day when he was riding along spying. The handlebars of the bike were full of rolled-up maps and messages. After that she married him with a good hiding from her father. She was bossy and gave him no chance.

Grandfather and Grandmother had big gardens at the back. Everybody helped there. Grandfather was tall and thin and a bit bent over from digging and weeding. But when he was young he was tall and straight and smiling in a soldier's uniform. He went to the second war and had his thumb blown away. His thumb got lost there, somewhere in a trench.

When Grandmother died that was when Mum came and married Dad. Mum saw Grandmother dressed up nice. Grandmother had the cloak and the pounamu. And she wore a little locket with tiny tiny photos of children. The children were Miria and Tame.

Well Dad remembered when he used to hikihiki Miria on his back, and he remembered Miria and Tame playing on the verandah and by the gardens. But Miria died of a disease in her back and Tame died of pneumonia when he had just learned to crawl.

And there were other babies of the whanau there too. Babies with real names but who had died before they got to be born. So it was as if they hadn't been born yet and come out and cry soon and want their kai. Or it was as if they were sleeping and waiting to be big enough to know you, and to come out and play, or to catch little fish with their quick hands, or to throw stones in the sea.

The children would weed the places and fill the jars with water, putting the same number of flowers in each jar to be fair. Then they would go from grave to grave squatting and putting an ear to each place. They would listen carefully but would hear nothing. No one called to them, no baby cried, no one whispered to them the secrets of under the ground.

'What colour are their kitchens?'

They stopped listening for the secrets of under the ground and sat up, looking at Manu. No one spoke for a long time.

'What colour are their kitchens?'

So Tangimoana said, 'Yellow. Their kitchens are yellow. And there aren't any windows. You can't see out or in. They sit all day and night in their kitchens, wrapped in blankets, and they mumble and stare. But there's really no day and night. And anyway they don't stay there all the time. Sometimes they crawl down skinny passages and bump their heads. They crawl and crawl, and sometimes they come to a free place where they sing and dance throwing their blankets down. They can step into water if they want to and swim down to a big whare whakairo with no need of breathing, where they talk all day long, but there's no real day. And Uncle Will has crawled back to Germany by now, but it's an underground Germany. He has maps and signs, and he meets grey people in the tunnels who sing in their throats. He never comes back to the yellow kitchen.'

'The babies.'

'The babies. Well the babies are not real yet. They are only wood without eyes and haven't had a chance. Not yet. But they're waiting . . . for something . . . their eyes to get put. And then . . . they'll pop up. Out of the ground. Or, out of the sea . . . yes, out of the sea. The sea will be red then . . . the sea was . . . red . . . that's all. Because we have to go home soon.'

'Soon, but we haven't told them things yet. We haven't said our things.'

'All right we'll have turns. James can go first and we can pick whoever we like.'

'All right, I pick my grandfather. "Tena koe e Koro. We never saw you because you dropped down dead in the garden and we weren't born then. But we've seen your photo at Granny Tamihana's. You were a soldier then in that photo but you still had your thumb. It was before you went. Your brothers and sisters, and you and Granny Tamihana's husband all used to work in the big gardens. Everyone worked there. And you all used to sell vegies by horse and cart, but mostly people couldn't pay. We all live in your house now, and we have other photos of you too. All the old things are still in the shed, and a bit rusty. Ko James ahau, tou mokopuna. Kia ora koe, e pa."'

'And I choose Miria and Tame. "Well Miria and Tame, I like it when we all crawl along the tunnels. Then we come out and throw our blankets down on the grass in the free place and dance and sing. Then we have a big swim and dive down to the big undersea houses and tutu round day and night, but there's no dark time and no shadows. You don't get lost. There's no eaters or snatchers, or doors that stay open half way. No bones to make rattle sounds by your windows, or by your eyes. We have a party sometimes, Miria and Tame, with Tangi, James and Toko and all our cousins. When I had my ear down I think I heard."'

'"Tena koe, Granny's brother. She said I could have your name. Eight people died in one month when you got born. Eight of our own whanau, because there was a bad sickness where we live. But you yourself, you did not die of a sickness, you died of a kehua. Granny was angry. She was a little girl then. But Granny gave me your name to help me, but it is not my only name. And she gave me a taonga from her ear to help me too. It is a taonga to help me in every way, but it is not the only taonga that I have. Ko Tokowaru-i-te-Marama koe, ko Tokowaru-i-te-Marama au. Kua mutu."'

'"Grandmother, I sleep in your room but it's all done out different now. I've got photos and books and a radio. There are yellow and red curtains and a blanket made of forty-seven different colours of wool that our Aunty Rina made for me. My mother and father were angry with me for cutting my name into the windowsill with a little knife – Tangimoana Kararaina Mary Tamihana. I do wrong things, not always. I get mad at Aunty Mary. I call her names, not always. Some teachers don't like me but some do. We have to go home soon and here is a song for you. It's about Granny's place. She's an older granny than you but you died before she did.

> "Seagulls walk on Granny's garden
> But one has a broken wing
> Seagulls walk with white white fronts
> But one is splashed with colour
> Seagulls walk close together
> But one looks at the sky
> Seagulls walk with flamy eyes
> But one steps in the fire."'

The children would pick up the containers while Manu held Toko's arm, then make their way slowly down the side of the hill without speaking. At the base of the hill they would always take the path to the sea that did not lead through the gardens or by the houses, instead they pushed their way through the lupins to the water.

They would wash the containers and then their hands and feet. They would clean the underneath of Toko's boots and flick water on each other. Then they would return to Granny's place and put the containers back under the shed.

Did you do this. Did you . . .? Yes Granny. Have you, have you? Yes. But Granny was not really angry.

'Haere mai mokopuna ma, ki te kai paraoa, ki te inu ti. Tomo mai ki roto. Kei te matemoe koutou? Kei te matekai koutou? Tomo mai ki roto.'

They would go into Granny's kitchen where the fire was always going and where the table would be set with best cups, and glass dishes of butter and jam. The big new round of bread would be on the board wrapped in a cloth.

'Tino pai o koutou mahi whakapaipai te urupa o te whanau. Tino pai hoki te whakarongo ki nga tono o to koutou kuia. E kai koutou, e kai. E inu hoki. . . .

19

Roimata

The seagulls cried above the land. They dipped and climbed and called, but there was no other sound as we set out with the boats.

Some went in the dinghies with the gear, and there was enough depth in the flood water to enable them to row, sometimes pole the boats along. Others of us made our way on higher ground round the side of the hills. We moved slowly because the way was slippery and steep. It was one of the young men walking ahead who turned and called that the creek was full of junk, but we didn't understand what he meant until we caught up with him and saw the heap of stone and concrete and bitumen showing above the flood water.

It is a small creek, and in places runs narrowly between sharp banks. Where it widens into pools there is not much banking at all. It was in a place where water from a shallow, bankless pool dropped into a narrow neck and flowed between steeply cut banks, that the dam had been made. But we did not realise at first that this damming had been deliberately done. Our first reaction was one of anger towards what we thought was the thoughtlessness, the lack of care, of those who made the roads.

Our next thought was to clear the blockage away quickly, to get the water moving again, because above all immediate thought was the knowledge that the banks of the urupa had begun to slip, and that our gardens were gone. These were the things that were heavy on us as we began to move the rubble away, piece by piece.

We were soon wet through and covered in mud as we levered rock and shovelled mud, as we dragged and lifted debris away from the channel. As we worked the thought came to me that this had been deliberately done.

Gradually we were able to make a narrow clearing so that the water began to flow again, slowly at first, and then more rapidly as we pulled away more and more of the rubble.

'They did this,' Stan said.

No one had spoken until then. There had only been the creening of the gulls.

'But why?'

We had all had the same thoughts.

'Getting back at us I suppose, or warning us to back off.'

I remembered the amount of money we'd been offered. I remembered the letter and its desperation, and knew that what Stan said was right.

'The urupa and the gardens,' someone said. 'They're trying to kill us.'

But we didn't speak of it any more just then. We continued with the work, shovelling mud and debris, passing rock and rubbish from hand to hand.

It was some time later that we saw a group of people making their way towards us. It turned out to be Matiu and Timoti and their three workmates, followed by Tangimoana and Tania. They had brought hot drink and food.

We set the kai down in one of the dinghies and stood about to drink the tea and eat the food that Matiu and the others had brought. We were too tired to speak of what had happened and why. The Matiu said, 'There's been a channel made, down the side of the hill,' but that was all he said.

Tangimoana was quiet, which was not usual. There was something to be told, but not by her.

'Korero, Son,' Hemi said.

'It's a channel. Been made to take the water down. To the urupa. Into it, where the soil has slipped.'

'Korero,' Hemi said again.

'Looking down from the road. You can see. Half hidden, but you can see. Put there, by . . . someone, to take the water down and do . . . harm. Someone from the job.'

'And all this too,' Hemi said. 'It took a man and a machine to do all this.'

'And. That's the finish for us,' Matiu said. 'We quit. There's a lot'll walk off once they know.'

He and Timoti and the other three men, as well as Tangimoana and Tania, took over the work that we'd been doing.

No one spoke then. We stood in silence about the dinghy,
our feet being pulled further and further into the mud of our
own turangawaewae, our own standing place. It was a world
of silence, an unfamiliar world, a world of other, a world
of almost drowning. We stood, not speaking, only trying to
search and sort the other, the almost drowning, to find a
pattern and a sense, to work through piece by piece to get
us home.

By the time we had finishẹd eating, the others had finished
clearing the creek. We picked up the gear, leaving the dinghies
where they were, and as we began making our way back
someone said, 'The ground is still the same ground.'

'The dead are still dead,' someone else said. 'And the living
are still on two feet.'

Much of the water was gone by then. There were people
about, and our family that had stayed behind was coming
in a slow procession to meet us at the urupa.

Above us the gulls were turning, eyeing the ground to which
they would occasionally drop in wauling groups before lifting
and circling again. The sky was clouded still, but it was high
white cloud, and the light showing through it caught the
undersides of the rising birds, and outlined the angled wing
shapes as they rose and wheeled, glinting and haloed above
the land.

'They've got Hoani with them,' Tangimoana said. 'And
there's those Pakehas who sat up on the road, well some of
them, helping to backy the kids through the mud.'

'And Granny, they're bringing her.'

'James. They rang James.'

We moved forward to greet them, to hold our most precious
ones to us – the little ones, and also those who were not strong
along with those who looked after them. And there was James
who had been away, and Hoani our minister who came whenever we needed him.

It was our own that were able to bring us home. It was
those who were not strong that could give us strength. The
mud that covered our bodies and our clothes now clung to

them as well, but it was the same mud that pulled at our feet, the mud of our own standing place.

'We know now someone did this,' Hemi said to Hoani. 'Our nephews told us what they found.'

'I understand you,' Hoani said. 'Nevertheless we must put all that aside. We must put the hurt aside, and we must approach the burial ground of the whanau without anger. Those other things . . . they are other matters. We will approach the damaged area together, the family, the friends. If there are visible remains, ka tika, we will not disturb them. What we are doing is that we are making the area safe and restful, so that if there is work that needs to be done then it can be done.'

Rina and James assisted Granny Tamihana as she led us forward calling to the spirits to go ahead of her, to be forward of us all on the path that we would all one day follow, and to be restful. Rina and James waited with her, while those of us who were able, climbed the hill about the broken area until we were surrounding it. Hoani moved up and about the slip, sluicing water from a bucket and reciting the karakia.

'Ka tika,' he said, when he had at last finished. 'All's well. Those that are at rest do so in peace and the earth holds them still. There is nothing needing to be moved, only that the earth that has broken away should be replaced.'

'Kei te pai e Pa. Ka tika.'

'The earth could be replaced today, and then whatever needs to be done for the safety of the area could be done tomorrow, or later. Then, whatever else needs to be thought about can be thought about.'

'Ka tika.'

We stood there quietly for some moments, then Granny began to chant a waiata, one that was known only to her. It spiralled thinly upwards, linking the earth that we are, to the sky that we are, joining the past that we are to the now and beyond now that we are. And when she had finished they helped her home.

'We'll do what we can now,' Stan said. 'And the rest can wait till tomorrow.' Those who had shovels moved in. We waited until the work was finished, then we, along with the

130

friends who had accompanied us, made our way home to wash and change and rest.

In the wharenui that evening there were many things to be discussed. We decided that we would ask for an official investigation because of what had been done. We asked Matiu and Timoti and the others not to leave their jobs. If the actions against us had been done deliberately in the hope of moving us, or of making us change our minds then we needed our own people there, 'to watch and listen', we said.

'But nothing to do with workers, or supervisors of work,' Matiu said. 'More like the top ones, the ones we don't see. Into bad business, so we hear. The big man does a fair bit of dealing. So we heard. And . . . the investigation, the police and that? They won't do nothing. Nothing good will come . . . for us. But anyway. All of us, we'll get back on the job, tomorrow. Or we'll come and give a hand cleaning up.'

'Kei te pai,' Rina said to them. 'You go back to work, we need you there. Leave tomorrow to us.'

But help did come the next day. At mid-morning Reuben and Hiria arrived with their youngest son Pena and four others from Te Ope. They had a small truck, and on it was work equipment and water pipes, and also meat and vegetables. Those who were at the wharenui made them welcome and they were soon out helping restore the urupa, and to clean up the houses that had been affected, and then to work in the area that had been our gardens.

And our livelihood.

'There's still the unemployment benefit,' someone said, making light of the fact that we would not now have an income from the land, and that we would now be short of kai.

'Never mind, he tangata,' someone else reminded us. 'We got people, ourselves as well as these others here. And the ground is still the same ground.'

'Like our own insurance company.'

131

Spirits were reviving.

Reuben and Hiria and the others stayed for a week, and during that time the urupa, the area where the gardens had been, and our houses, were all cleaned up and made safe should there be heavy rain again.

During that time Pena fell in love with Tangimoana but she was not ready to be in love with anyone.

'I need him though,' she said. 'And that might be almost the same.'

Pena thought it was enough and they have been together much of the time since then.

In the evenings the Te Ope people talked about their struggles of the past, of their new work, and of their hopes and dreams. They were not new stories to us, except that stories are always new, or else there is always something new in stories.

We told of our work, and of our dreams too, and discussed also the new threat to our lives which was the threat of money and power. Except that money and power were not a new threat. Money and power, at different times and in many different ways, had broken our tribes and our backs, and made us slaves, filled our mouths with stones, hollowed the insides of us, set us at the edge and beyond the edge, and watched our children die.

But when Reuben heard a name, he said, 'That's the same one isn't it, who was in the news a while back, two or three years ago? Had his Jag bombed. They say it was in retaliation for his lot burning the Bowder Street nightclub. Didn't get done for it though, or even charged. Only got his Jag blown up. It was meant to have him in it when it blew, but didn't. That's what I heard. Dangerous man I'd say, and he's got his people, that's for sure.'

Everything we need is here. Hemi is right to say it. But because it is so, and because we have been busy surviving, we have lost much of our interest in matters outside of here. But Reuben is a man who is in touch with a wider world. We were fearful of whatever else could happen.

And the people of Te Ope spoke of James, 'your mokopuna', they called him. 'He is giving part of his young life to us,' they said, 'just as all of you have given us your aroha in the past. When he rang back to tell us what had happened we packed up and came, and that's what we will always do.'

During that week others came too. There were the friends who had come on the first day, there were neighbours, and there were family returning from other places. They helped with the work and brought their koha to us. Often after work Matiu and Timoti would come and they would always have others with them.

One night when the meeting-house was full of people Toko leaned towards me and said, 'These are the people of hunger and anger that will come when everything is grown and green.'

His face was hot and his hair was damp but he was not, just then, in pain. I moved him on to my knee, though he was not a child any longer, and he put his face against my hair.

'The stories have changed,' he said. He was weary as he leaned against me, and his words came slowly. 'And there's a night of colours. And also a night of stars.'

An investigation was held but this mostly consisted of a questioning of us and our observations, and a criticism of our actions. We should not have removed the material that had allegedly dammed the creek. We should not have fixed the slip at the cemetery or put in drains. So the enquiry showed that a dam had possibly been made, that a channel had possibly been deliberately formed down the side of the hill, and that flooding had occurred, but that was all.

20

Toko

On the night of colours I awoke to a night of sounds. There's a story of colours and it is also a story of sounds.

They were not new sounds, at first. They were the sounds of my brother Manu shouting and crying in his sleep, and of my birth mother Mary singing in her room.

I did not open my eyes. I did not get up to wake my brother as I had always done when we were children. I did not get into bed beside him. My body was slow by then and I knew that I should not put strain on my growing heart. I knew not to get up in the night without someone to assist me. I called to my brother instead of going to him, but he did not wake or stop his calling.

I pulled the blanket from my face to call to Mary, but Mary did not hear me and did not stop her singing. And on opening my eyes I found that there was no darkness in the room. The night was light and full of dancing colours.

'Hemi,' I called. 'Roimata, Tangi, James.'

Then suddenly, in the night of ordinary sounds there were other sounds. Doors were opening, and slamming shut. There was calling and running on the paths and roadways. My parents and Tangi and James were running out of the house. People of the whanau were shouting and running, out into the night that was day-bright and filled with colour.

'Mary wake him,' I called. 'Mary help me,' but she did not hear. I rolled to the edge of my bed and put my feet to the floor. I turned, seating myself on my brother's bed and shaking him. 'Wake up, wake up,' I said.

'Don't get up,' he said.

'Wake up. Listen to the people.'

'I am awake. I hear them, but it isn't real.'

'Wake up,' I said. 'It's real. Listen to the people and look at the orange night.'

My brother got out of his bed and went to the window.

'The wharenui is on fire,' he said. 'And the people are running to the sea. They're crying and shouting, and beating at the flames. But it isn't real,' he said.

'It is. It's real. Wake up.'

'It won't be real.'

'Wake up and go and help them.'

There were sirens in the night of sounds.

'Help them?' he asked.

'Yes help. Go. . . . '

'Who?'

'The people. Hemi, Roimata, Tangi, James. . . . Help them . . . put the fire out.'

'We're all burning,' he said, 'But it won't be real. You wake and . . . nothing's real.'

'Take me,' I said. 'Come on help me.' I pulled a rug over myself and edged into my chair. 'Put your jacket on and help me.'

Manu wheeled me out of the house and down the path as the engines went by. 'The sirens,' he said. 'Burning. Burning in the night, but then . . . nothing. Nothing's real.'

Ahead of us Mary was running, in her own shuffling way, and she was calling and crying, 'Oh don't! Don't go! Don't go away from Mary!'

And then Manu began to shout too, 'It is! It is! Oh it's real! We're all awake, and it's real! Fire is here, and burning!'

'Leave me,' I said. 'Go and help them.'

'People are making chains to the sea.'

'Leave me and join them,' I said.

He left and I began to wheel myself slowly along in the shouting, crying, daylit colour night, towards the house of people. The timbers cracked like shot, and thudded into the orange burning like the falling of trees.

And there was fire too, on the inside of me, burning and changing me, because fire does always cause to change whatever it feeds upon. Yet fire, in the beginning, had been gift-given, seeds of it springing from the topknot and into the heart of trees – not imprisoned but only hidden there, awaiting the breath and the touch.

I made my way slowly to where my birth mother Mary had sat herself on the roadway rocking and crying and calling out, 'Come back. Oh Boyboy they going away from me. Loving and singing people. Oh going away, oh Boyboy going away from me.'

The firemen were running with the hoses, jetting the water into the flames, but the roof had gone. The great head of the great ancestor that looked out towards the people whenever they advanced across the marae had gone. The arms that had been extended in welcome, and the sacred and intricate backbone that had run through the apex, as well as the patterned ribs adjoining the backbone, had caved, and dropped into the flames, and gone.

The walls had fallen too, taking and changing the tipuna of the people – the loving, warring, singing, talking, shouting guardians of the night and day. Taking also the patterns belonging to the lives and deaths of people, the stories and histories of people, and the work of hands and minds. Taking the people's place of resting, their place of learning, of discussing, singing, dancing, sorrow, joy, renewal, and whanaungatanga. Taking the world inside which all else may be left behind, as dust is left on shoes beyond the door.

The water from the hoses played over the flattened, smoking remnants of the ancestral house, and the sounds became silence. The night became dark.

We could only stand silent in the night's silence and in the night's darkness. It was as if we were the new tekoteko figured about the edges of the gutted house, unhoused, standing in place of those that had gone to ash.

There had not been a darker night or one more quiet. We moved to the wharekai to wait for morning. For a long time no one spoke but sat quietly and wept, and the tears were tears that went right back into the past of living memory and also into the distant past of only spoken memory. But the tears were also for the now, and for the future time.

After a long time someone said that the house had gone but that we still had people, and we had the ground. 'And you build from people and you build from the ground.' But the words did not give comfort. No one else spoke.

Instead we began to sing, which is a way of saving your soul, or the centre of you. It was a quiet and restful singing of melodies and harmonies circling in the increasing light that came to the wharekai, but which could not be made to rise above our eyes, and there was little comfort in it.

Right then it was not comfort enough, and my sister stood up and shouted above the singing. 'Those bastards next door did this,' so we stopped singing. 'And I'll get them for this. Somehow.'

'We'll get it . . . looked into,' someone said.

'And this time, won't touch anything.' But they were only saying it to calm her. 'An investigation should show. . . .'

'Fuck the investigation. What did that show last time? Told us nothing. Told us probably this probably that. Probably. Not "it did". Not "who did". Not "he did, she did". Nothing. Fuck the enquiry. I know what it'll find and you know what it'll find. It'll find we did it ourselves. They'll go through all their shit and rubbish and try and hang it on us. Like last time. And. Who was last in the house yesterday? Aunty Mary, right? What're they going to presume when they get that bit of information? When they find out it was her, Aunty Mary, that was last in there, what do you think they will all have buzzing round in their small, shitty screwed around minds?'

No one spoke. We knew what would be in their minds.

'Those Pakeha friends of ours knew what they were doing when they chainsawed tyres and bowled the shed over the bank. It should have been us doing that. Especially since it was thought we did it anyway. It was insinuated. . . . Should have been us putting the chainsaw through. And, one of these days . . . soon. . . . And if none of yous help me then it'll just be me . . . all by my own black self.'

None of us spoke, only sat, heavily, thinking about all that had happened and all that had been said. Fire causes to change what it touches, and yet it was, in the beginning, gift-given.

When daylight came we went out to look at the ruin that had been the house of genealogies, of living and dying and dreams. Mary had gone out ahead of us and was standing amongst the disintegrated timbers pulling a scarred and blackened poupou from the pile.

Our lives, our stories, had changed. Fire bursts at the feet and engulfs the world, and even the beat-winged bird cannot climb above it, but must call and cry for rain.

21

Toko

We did not work in the gardens at all that day, even though
it was the busy season. I could not work in the gardens on
any day, but I could be there, and be useful in many ways.
I could sort seed, or count out the little plants ready for
transplanting, and I could label boxes, bags and trays.

We stood looking at the remains of the house for a long
time, then when Granny Tamihana turned away to go back
to the wharekai we followed her.

'What shall we do?' someone said, but no one answered,
not Tangimoana, not any of us, not for a long time.

Then Granny Tamihana said, 'Manaakitia te manuhiri,'
and we became aware of people, the friends who had come
when the land had flooded. And there were police and newspaper people and members of the fire brigade. 'Look after
the visitors.'

We began to move round, rolling the white paper on to
the tables, cutting bread, putting the water on to boil, taking
cups from the cupboard, but we did not think about any of
these things as we did them. Our bodies moved, our hands
moved, doing the familiar things, but our thoughts, our
spirits, were in ruin, fallen to broken earth.

As we worked no one spoke, could not speak, not Tangimoana, not any of us, except occasionally Granny Tamihana.

I can look back to that time and I can remember that it
was the old lady Tamihana who moved to and fro, who filled
the Zip with water, who began taking the cups from the cupboards, doing the things that the younger ones would usually
do. It was the old lady and not Aunty Rina who said to put
out the cups, toast some bread, set up the table, put the water
on to boil, look after the visitors.

And I can look back to that time and know that it was

then, listening to Granny and watching her move about the wharekai, that I really understood her stories. For all of my life up until then I had listened to all her stories, stories which she always told with a kind of joyfulness. But it was then as she took the cups down, filled the Zip, took the spoons from the drawer, that I really understood that her life had truly been a life of loss and sorrow, and that loss and sorrow were ordinary in her life.

As a young girl, the hills where she had learned the use of plants, and known the trees and birds that lived there, had gone to others.

She had lost her most loved and only brother, and later had outlived her husband, all of her children, and some of her grandchildren as well. She had seen grandchildren and great-grandchildren leave and not return, or return broken and ill, only to leave again.

As a young woman she had been robbed and mistreated by those whose floors she had scrubbed. And as a young woman she had seen her children go hungry and cold, because although there had been government payments for others during the bad times after the first war, there had not been such benefits for people of our race. She had watched her children die.

She had been barred from places where those not of our race had been allowed to go freely, the landscape about her had continually changed, the sounds about her had changed – and now the sacred house, built not long after she was born, had gone in fire.

I really understood for the first time that to Granny, loss and grief were ordinary and expected. I saw that pain was so ordinary, and sorrow so ordinary, that they were close, so close, to being almost joy – a kind of silent, shouting, gruelling ecstacy, as opposites turn near to each other on the many-stranded circle. She had known for eighty years that kicking the casket does not jolt the dead brother back to life.

So it was she who led us to do the usual things of making tea, putting the cups out, bringing those who were outside in, pouring the tea from the big teapots, and then gradually to discuss what had happened, telling what we knew to those who had come.

The remainder of that day was taken up with people coming, and us telling what we knew, telling what we did. The next day we began to talk to each other about what should be done, and then we went to begin the cleaning up. My sister Tangimoana had not yet come to the ordinary things. She was quiet, as yet unable to help with the ordinary things.

Hoani began our day with karakia to put evil away and rightness before us. 'We must have rightness with us,' he said. 'We must look after our good health, which is a health of spirit and a health of people. The life spirit of each one of us must be cared for – the people looking after the one. And the life spirit of the people must be cared for, the one supporting the whole.

'We must have a clear mind and a right way,' he said, 'Because wrongness comes back to the wrongmaker. I believe it. It's something to remember.'

My sister who was standing by me did not look up when he spoke the words, but turned and walked away. Before we could begin work we stood about the gutted house to poroporoaki – farewelling all that it had housed, and all that it had meant to all of us.

We began then to sort through the burnt timbers, but I could not help, could only watch, there was little that I could do. There was nothing that could be saved apart from the partially burnt poupou that my birth mother Mary had pulled from the rubble the day before, and which she had kept by her since.

We did not remove the debris from the site but instead made a trench and buried it there, so that the new could spring from the old which is the natural way of things. That's what old Hoani said.

It was hard work and took all day to complete, and when it was finished everyone went down to the lagoon to wash the fire-black from bodies and clothes. I had not been able to work much, but I joined them in the water which was cool and salt.

Tangimoana joined us too, even though she had not

worked, had not been with us all day, and had not come yet to the ordinary things. But she came down and lay on the sea, which stings the wound but at the same time heals.

It was while we were in the sea that we saw a vanload of people arrive. The van was followed by a truck with a load on the tray. The two vehicles stopped by the marae entrance, and the people waited there until we could be ready to receive them. We knew that it was Reuben and Hiria, and others from Te Ope.

We put our towels about us and went to our houses for clean clothes, then went on to our marae ground to call our visitors to us. It was a sad thing to stand in the place where we had so often stood when welcoming our manuhiri, and not to feel our wharenui standing strongly behind us.

The visitors came to us, standing for a long time at the centre of the marae to tangi with us over those who had died in the past and what had been lost now.

Then the speeches of welcome began, speeches during which our visitors were told of all that had happened, and what we believed were the reasons for what had happened. We told them what we had done that day so that the new could grow from the old in the natural way of things.

In their replies they told us that they were there to help and support us as we had helped and supported them in the past. They were there to help rebuild, and to work for as long as we needed them.

'We have brought our tents with us,' Reuben said. 'Tents are now a part of our history and part of our lives. They are part of the identity of Te Ope, part of our pride.'

There had been such silence up until then, a moving from one ordinary thing to another, but now, suddenly, there was singing again, and talking, and noise in the wharekai, and laughter too.

We helped the visitors to put up the tents which had become part of their identity and pride. The next day a workshop was constructed and planning for the new house began.

And from then on many people came. Some stayed a day, some a week, others stayed days, or weeks. Each one brought gifts – of food or equipment, or materials. Tradespeople and craftspeople came with their various skills. Money arrived, along with letters of encouragement and support from maraes all round the country. There were people all over the country who understood what those undertaking the investigation did not understand. They understood that the house of the people is a great taonga and a great strength. They understood that the little money that was finally awarded to us could not give back the life and love that go into the making of a place, could not give back the life of trees. They understood, no matter what the reports had said, or left unsaid, that a deliberate act would have been the same as turning one's hand against oneself.

There were enough people amongst us who were experienced planners and builders, and construction of the new house was soon underway. However there were new skills to be learned, or skills that were new to us, skills that had not been used in our area since Granny was young. We had never had to collect pingao before, and never had to seek out, and use, the black mud dye. But our Granny Tamihana has a memory for places and a knowledge of what grows and what the uses are of the various plants. Also, our visitors had more recently been involved in the building of a house and could show us what to do.

Our beach and our little piece of bush did not have the pingao and kiekie that we needed for the tukutuku work – or not, at that stage, in quantity. We had to go on several excursions to collect the materials. Shelters that were airy yet dry had to be erected so that the pingao and kiekie could be hung and allowed to dry there.

We were all caught up in the excitement of planning, building and decorating the new house, of working out designs and patterns, and watching these grow. Some of the patterns and designs followed the old ones, these being already part of ourselves. They were etched on the memory and were patterns of the stars and the sea, of the fish and birds and plants, and also of learning and relationships, conflict, sorrow and joy. But there were new patterns too, of flooding and fire, roads and machines, oneness and strength, and work and growth.

We were caught up, both in the excitement, and in the exhaustion of working from daybreak until dark, and then after dark. Because there were still the gardens to work during daylight hours and still the fishing to be done, although I could not, by then, go fishing or work on the land, and was not allowed to exhaust myself the way that others did.

'Build something, and it builds you,' was what Hoani said, and I thought of a long time ago when the old lady had said to me, 'You know what I do, I make myself.' And she had given me the little kit which I have still. 'It's myself, to give,' she'd said. 'And your big fish, it's yourself, to give.'

I could sit comfortably in my chair close to the tukutuku frames, often with my sister Tangimoana on the opposite side, and taking the strips of pingao or kiekie, crosswork the half-round sticks to the backboard. As the strands worked to and fro so did our stories, so did what we had in our hearts and minds. We sang to and fro, latticing down and along the strips of black, red, white and gold, which had become the strands of life and self.

Among those who had come from Te Ope, along with his tools and his skills, was their carver, an old man who had taught what he knew to others of his whanau, as well as to my brother James. Carving was not work that I could do but two of my cousins took it up. Also, young carvers from other areas joined us too, people with a keenness to learn and a willingness to give their time towards helping replace what had been destroyed.

Gradually the new figures emerged from wood, and these figures were not new in name because ancestry remains, but they were new in appearance. What was brought forward this time, from trees, came forward under different eyes and from under different hands.

There was hardship greater than we had known it before as we shared what we had with those who had come to our assistance. There was exhaustion as the family went about the daily work in the gardens or kitchen, as they caught the fish and collected the seafood needed for all of the people. And often there was not enough. Then after the day's work people returned from the gardens and came from the kitchens to join the builders, carvers, weavers, painters and pattern-makers, who had also been working at their tasks since early morning.

Our work occupied us so intensely that we could try not to be distracted by the blasting of the hills and the shore rock, and could turn away from the walling and confining and spoiling of the sea. We could easily ignore the further requests that we sell our land, or lease it, or site our new house differ-ently, or centrally, so that the new would not have sprung from the old in the proper way of things.

Everything we need is here, but for some years we had had little contact with other people as we struggled for our lives and our land. It was good now to know new people and to feel their strength. It was good to have new skills and new ideas, and to listen to all the new stories told by all the people who came. It was good to have others to tell our own stories to, and to have them there sharing our land and our lives. Good had followed what was not good, on the circle of our days.

22

Hemi

The sun would not go down for another hour yet, and even after that there would still be enough light to work by for a while. It was setting further round now, getting down a lot earlier. Each year you noticed it at about this time – suddenly.

On most days they worked until they could no longer see, but that day Hemi had told them to pack up the gear and take it to the shed. He'd told them to go and have a kai because he felt sorry for them, felt aroha for them. Not just for the ones who had been out with him from early morning, but also for those who had come for the morning, or afternoon, fitting garden work in amongst other tasks. He felt concern for them, especially for the young ones, felt concern that their young lives were being spent bent over the land.

Like himself. At their age he'd worked like that. Had to. But it seemed he'd chosen it, or been chosen for it. And he'd always been strong, and . . . different. Perhaps different, he wasn't sure. Well. He'd never had time to be young, to do things other young people did because there was always work. But on the other hand he'd always seen the gardens as his thing to know about and be good at. He'd liked it all right – the first quick shootings in the spring, and the largeness of summers filled with fat leaves and heavy fruit and creeping bees. Probably because he was a stick-in-the-mud who never looked past his nose.

But he didn't want to see these young ones breaking their backs, even though it was for . . . survival, getting enough food and a bit of money to keep them all. Then again if you looked at the other side of it, at least they could say they'd seen the fruits of their work, and that the fruit they got was their own. Different from working for a boss where you stayed poor anyway, stayed poor and made someone else rich.

It had been a good season. They'd had good caulis, cab-bages big as wheels, beans had come wide, like straps on the plants, and there'd been large crops of potato and kumara. He'd shown them how to make a kumara pit like the old-time ones, and they'd put a good store away. The pumpkin, kamokamo and marrow had flowered early and they'd sent truckload after truckload to market. Lettuces had come quickly to crisp heads, and tomatoes had fattened and red-dened on good big stalks. Then there were the rows of carrots and peppers, silverbeet, beetroot and onions. In the water channels the watercress had grown thick and tall. Then every-thing had slowed down a bit with summer all but gone, and now it was time to prepare the ground for the next lot.

It had nearly busted them getting things going again after all that water. That was a hard one. But they'd had good help. People always turned up when you needed them most. They'd all wondered what would happen when the next big rain came, but it was okay, it turned out good. The job they'd done on the land had made it safe, and Timoti and Matiu had stayed on at their jobs and were keeping their eyes open. Too busy to feel resentment over it all, but dig deep enough and the resentment would be there jabbing at his liver, or somewhere, if he stopped to think.

Especially after the next blow, which was a killer. Very hard. You had to somehow get through it. Pull others through too. You had to remember that it's the people and the land that survive, and you had to watch the old lady carrying on with . . . life, so you could remember the things you'd always believed in.

But his daughter had taken it bad, and no one blamed her either because it had shaken them all up. And she could be right, wanting to . . . get in. As for himself, he just couldn't find it in himself to be destructive – against people. People were the most important thing in life, he believed. Although she reckoned it wasn't against people. 'Against things,' she'd said, 'for the sake of people. Doesn't mean I want to kill anyone . . . yet. And we don't have to *expect* do we? We don't have to wait for it, think we deserve it, think it's our lot, or think it won't happen again. It doesn't stop. I mean it's all happened before, hasn't it? It's the same things. The same, all the time. Don't you see?'

Well she shook you up all right. Dearest daughter. There were some who would say she was becoming lost to them. Would say that the ways she had learned away from there were not good ways, not their own ways. They'd say she was doing the same things as those she spoke against. But he knew his daughter was no different from what she'd always been. It was curiosity that always moved her, then after that it was love, a love that was a kind of anger.

And it was love and anger, as well as sorrow, that pulled at him, would turn him, if he let it.

Because he who had been happy to live a life with people and just be part of them, who had found all he wanted in a time and place, and who had never doubted, now felt . . . a shifting, that he did not want to acknowledge. He did not want anger, or sorrow to turn him . . . against people. It wasn't his way. In his whole life he had never kept anger in him, against people. Now . . . it was hard. Now, it was the soil that saved him, the need to feed the whanau. And there it was again. People. People needing people. Tangi-moana wouldn't agree with driving feelings into the soil, digging over the loss and hurt, just struggling day to day. 'The minute you're born,' she'd said to him, 'your nose is in the ground. But I'll die, no sweat, if I can do it saying I'm me, and knowing that someone believes it. I'll die without a kick if I can have a feather in my hair.'

A feather. Well he wasn't sure. It sounded wrong. He'd tried to say things to her, to help with . . . anger. Tried to dig her anger in, alongside his own. But no, Tangi had just shifted . . . from loud to quiet, that's all. Then after a while she'd gone, and so far hadn't contacted them. Pena had gone to get her but she'd sent him away.

It was almost dark. He stopped work and began to collect the vegetables that would be needed for the next day. He worked slowly, cutting the cabbages, pulling the carrots and onions and putting them into the barrow. There he was, alone with his thoughts and dilemmas, two generations removed from the old lady on the one hand, another generation removed from his kids on the other, and it was like being on a swing.

Something to talk to Reuben about perhaps. Reuben had had his go when he was a kid sitting on the land, and he'd waited a long time before any of the older ones had gone there and supported him. They could be letting Tangimoana down trying to keep her from hurt, trying to lessen her feelings and her anger, but it just wasn't in him to match fire with fire.

And back to his first thoughts. Could the young ones stick it out on the land, the ones there now, because some had gone already. Come, gone. When the jobs had got tight they'd come home, a lot of them. Tried to stick with it, but they were too . . . broken, to make a go of it. Had already had the stuffing taken out of them, and couldn't last out. Made him feel bad too, as though he'd let them go, made them go, expected too much. And now these ones, the stayers, he felt . . . sad, about their young lives. He felt aroha for them. Didn't know if he should expect them to work the way he'd worked at that age, day after day, month after month, and probably year after year.

He could be, in the end, driving their own young ones away. The kids too, the little ones. They had to do more in a day than he liked to see them do. Out there bending their backs for whole days at a time in some seasons, but how would they manage without? Didn't know what they'd have done without their kids sometimes, or without the help that had come. And there you are, it all came back to people. Full circle, that was something he could believe in.

Then again there was something else niggling at him that Tangimoana had said. 'People?' she'd said. 'Yes, but some people aren't people. They've forgotten how.'

Well the real ones, then. People had come and people had sent letters and koha. They'd all pulled together and the house was being rebuilt because of that. You had to reach out for the branch you *knew* would hold you when you were drowning.

And you could only do your best, the best that you knew. He wanted all the whanau back, wanted to be sure that everything they needed was there. And it was up to him to make sure it was, that was how he felt. It was all leaning on him.

Well last night someone had come, he didn't know who. Sat on him, heavily. On his chest as he half slept. Frightened him too, and he'd had it on his mind all day. Didn't know what it meant and didn't know who. Perhaps he wasn't doing things right. Or it could have been a warning. Someone come to tell him something . . . but about what? Surely they'd had enough. 'Ko wai tenei?' he'd asked into the dark. 'He aha to pirangi?' But there'd been no sound, no reply, only weight which held him so that he couldn't move.

A warning? But what more could happen? He didn't want to think of what more could happen. . . . He would say nothing to anyone, because no good could come of talking about it just now. Only more for them to worry about. One day he would talk about it. For now he would just live with it, try to think only about what was the right thing for him, for people, the ones here, the ones gone. All he could do now was what he'd always done, or tried to do – keep the home warm.

The outside world would turn, faster and faster, he supposed, and in what direction he couldn't tell. But his world, the one he knew and understood, was there just the same, to hold if he could. The same, except that sometimes the self could shift. Who had come to him in the night, and what did it mean?

He trundled the barrow towards the wharekai which was all lit and full of sounds. And there were lights on in the workshop too, as people set up to work for a few more hours.

He left the barrow by the door of the wharekai and made his way towards the wash-room.

23

Roimata

The stories had changed. It was as Toko had said, the stories had changed. And our lives had changed. We were living under the machines, and under a changing landscape, which can change you, shift the insides of you.

Above all we lived under the threat and destructiveness of the power people, and we had only really begun to understand the power.

Before the burning of the house we had known and felt our own strength, which had come from knowing ourselves, and from knowing a direction. But after that time, the time of the fire, we began to really live with fear, and with a question in our minds as to what else could happen, what else could be done in an attempt to destroy us. Was the strength of our own feet enough? Was it enough to have feet on ground? 'Because it's not ordinary,' Reuben warned. 'Not just a dirty game. They've found money won't shift you and they'll want to push you off, frighten you, get you off somehow. We mustn't think it's just a dirty game that they'll become tired of sooner or later. They can't help it, can't stop. Can't think, because they have become just like their machines.'

Yet I am a patient watcher of the skies. We worked so hard that summer, which was a summer of long, fine days and of hot, heavy work. The gardens flourished and the new house went up. In spite of the threat in our lives there was excitement about, and energy.

Our visitors, who had been away from their homes for several months by then, must have been anxious to go home. What they were doing for us would never be forgotten, though to them what they were doing was simply a return for support we had given them in the past.

They stayed because they knew what it meant to the spirit

and upliftment of people to be housed in a house which expressed and defined them. They knew what those who had conducted the enquiry had not known, that for us to have destroyed our own house would have meant an end with no new beginning, a nothingness – earth nothing, sky nothing, nothing in the belly of the sea, a return to the nothing where nothing stirs.

But I am a patient sky watcher, and there was not, after all, nothing. In amongst the debris our very dearest Mary had sat, with her man. She had pulled him from the ash, put her ear against his chest, and begun, softly, to sing.

So Mary and her man were the first new breath. People coming in trucks were the second. From there had come a growth and a flourishing, a leaping from within the dark sea, a deep and excited breathing.

At another level there was pain. We had not forgotten what had happened, what had been done. We could not ignore the falling rock, the levelling of land, the arrival of materials, the new yellow colour of the sea.

And Tangimoana had gone. She had not phoned or written, had hardly said goodbye. She did not agree with our acceptance of a situation, which was not a deep-down acceptance, but only a waiting one. She saw the strength of a bending branch to be not in its resilience, but in its ability to spring back and strike.

24

Toko

There is a special door that was made for me and my chair. It is a door at the side of the new wharenui specially hinged so that it opens either out or in. There is a ramp and a wide pathway from the road to enable me to come and go easily. It was not easy by then, for me to be without my chair.

My uncles planned and built the special door for me, and the people made the ramp and path. My brother James carved the doorway, and in his carvings told the special story of the joining. It is the story of how our people had become as one with the people of Te Ope.

To do this my brother had looked back in the genealogies until he found a common ancestress from whom both people could show descent. He carved the head and shoulders of this ancestress at the centre of the door lintel, showing her to face both out and in. The two thick, strong arms of the woman stretched out to embrace the two poles that made the door frames on either side. Down these two poles the people were interspersed, the people of our iwi and the people of Te Ope, but linked at the top of the columns by the woman. It was her children that she clasped at either side of her. And these children were working, laughing, crying, singing people, some small and some larger than life. They were young and old, and were joined by their fingers or toes, hands, feet, arms, legs, foreheads or tongues until all had become part of one another. They faced to the hills on the outside, and on the other side they looked in.

It is a beautiful door that opens without noise. Inside the door and to the left of it was my mattress covered by a rug, which was left there all the time for me, and there was a space beside my mattress for my chair.

Once inside the house someone would help me onto my

mattress, and I could wrap warm in my rug. I could listen
to what I wanted to listen to, and if I wished to speak, or
was asked to speak, I could speak from there, throwing my
voice high into the heke. I was always given a time to speak
even though speaking is mostly done by those who are old.
But the people knew that I would never be old, and that is
why they allowed me oldness while I was a child still. Some
would say that I had never been a child.

I could sit or sleep right there beneath the carving-man/
loving-man made complete again, his new feet resting on my
head. Because there hadn't, after all, been nothing. It was
my own mother Mary who had sat amongst the water-soaked
ruins of the first house and pulled the loving-man from the
ash. She had held him to her, put her ear to his heart, and
had begun, softly, to sing.

I had helped her to clean the ash and marks away, and
under the dust we'd found the little watching eyes, the talking
tongue, the other mallet-heart. We'd found, just faintly, the
pattern of scarves, and found the hand that clasped the handle
of the lifing chisel – but the broadened, figured, penis end
of the chisel had burned away. The feet and legs of the man
had gone, fire having gone mostly to the groin.

This poupou, found in the dust by my first mother Mary,
was the link from old to new, that's what everyone said. It
was the piece that showed that there had been no real death,
or showed perhaps that death is a coiled spring. This piece
had been the last one carved for the old house, but had not
been completed even then. And it became the first piece for
the new house, which meant we were able in our new house
to show a linking from the man who had no children of his
own, and a linking from before that through him, connecting
all of us to the great and ancient ancestor whose name the
house had been given.

And the man who had no children had been gifted down
in wood by one who had represented himself in a pattern from
scarves, even though he'd been told not to show a living
memory, by one who had chosen, at the end of his life, to
do what he had been told never to do – to give breath to wood.
It had all been told in stories from when Granny was a little

girl, when the man grown out of his frailty had built a house for the people. He had brought out of wood a living memory, then he'd given his breath.

He had left the lower half of the poupou untouched, a place for the mokopuna of the man who had no children of his own.

And that was the place given to me to sit, keeping warm the place of the child not by then known. I could be, for a while, the mokopuna, the one not yet shown in wood.

It was a quiet place for me. I could listen there, or rest. Because I had been given special oldness I could speak from there to the heke, or to the quiet, waiting hearts.

One night Roimata and I went out to look for Manu, and found him sitting under the new doorway. 'There's fire,' he said, but Roimata told him there was no fire. 'That was before,' she said, and tried to wake him, tried to make him see. He did not wake, did not see, but we took him back home to bed where he slept quietly for the rest of the night.

PART THREE

25

Roimata

The hills are quiet and the machines have been taken away. After a while the trees will begin to grow again and soon the water will be clear. There is comfort in knowing these things, but is there enough comfort? Good can come from what is not good, good can come from sorrow, new life from old, but is it enough? Hemi and I will put down the nets again and we will have butterfish and moki. We will fish from the dinghies or from the shores. We will have clean mussels from the reef when the water is clear.

All that we need is here, Hemi says. It's true and there's comfort in knowing it, but is there enough comfort, even considering that I am, have always been, an ever-patient watcher of the skies? We have known what it is to have had a gift, and have not ever questioned from where the gift came, only sometimes wondered. The gift has not been taken away because gifts are legacies, that once given cannot be taken away. They may pass from hand to hand, but once held they are always yours. The gift we were given is with us still.

His death had been with us a long time but not the manner of it. The manner of his death, that is where the pain is – the manner of his death, and the brokenness and suffering of the little bird. His death brought Tangimoana back to us, brought others to us, gave us much that is good, but is it enough, can it be enough?

Tangimoana would not sit at his side during the time of mourning. She went alone that first day, up to the workplace in the hills. 'You've killed my brother,' she said. 'You've killed our own brother, my own brother who, when I was a child, I saved from drowning.'

'He hasn't been here,' they said, some of them moving away to begin their work.

'You bled the land,' she shouted, and those who had been about to move remained. 'And you almost destroyed the sacred place in a time of rain. You fired our first house and now you've killed our brother.'

'He's not here,' one said.

'Hasn't been here.'

And another said, 'Don't come here shouting, you can't blame those things. . . .'

But another said, 'What do you mean about your brother?'

'He's dead and you did it. You, you, all of yous.' And she began telling them about her brother.

While she was telling, Matiu and Timoti left and came running down from the hills and have not been back there since, except once. And when she had finished telling they were all quiet.

'It's bad,' someone said.

'We know your . . . feelings. But us. . . .'

'We work. . . .'

'Just a job. . . .'

'For money. . . .'

'And kai.'

They were all silent for a long time, then Tangimoana said, 'It's true what you say, but I want to blame . . . it's how I feel . . . to stop from crying. There's no time for crying. But I said it also to make you listen to me. Yous have to listen to me, you're the only ones who can help. Yous have to listen to me, and understand, and believe me. When I've told everything to you, and when you think back to all what you've heard, then yous'll know and yous'll believe me, and yous'll understand.

'Well the enquiries and investigations that we had did not show that what I'm saying to you is true, and an enquiry will not be likely to show the truth this time either. But we know. Us living on the land, we know. I want yous to know. You're all here for a job like you said. And yous are the only ones who can believe . . . not high-up people. High-up people are evil, and . . . blind. They're weak . . . and doomed.'

160

The men did listen to her. It's a way Tangimoana has, a sharp boldness that will make people listen to her. Also it is a way of hers to act alone.

The machines were not heard that day on the hills, and have not been heard since, except once. Many of the men who walked down off the hills that morning were of our own race but some were not. They had listened to and understood and believed what Tangimoana had said to them, and had come to bring their aroha and their koha to us and to our child.

They stayed with us throughout the three days, helping us with the visiting people that came. People came in hundreds. It was a comfort to have such crowds of people coming to be with us and our child, our precious one, our potiki. It was comforting, and yet in one respect there could be no comfort. It was exhausting too, but exhaustion was something to be thankful for.

Tangimoana spent the nights sleeping beside her brother, but during the three days she was out amongst the people with Pena alongside her, working in the wharekai. Which is not the usual way, but Tangimoana acts alone. 'I want them to know,' was all she would say, 'I want them to believe and to understand. And I want to know who are the ones who believe and understand, and who are the ones who don't.'

We did not question her.

At the final karakia for our child the marae was full. It was a warm day, and although there was fine rain we took our potiki out onto the marae for the karakia, so that everyone could be accommodated. There were more people on our marae that morning than I have ever seen. There was much comfort in seeing it, but for some things there is little comfort. We were glad of exhaustion.

It was a painful thing when the lid went down taking our child from our sight, our child along with his pendant and his basket, but he had other gifts as well.

It was a painful thing to follow the polished casket, walking slowly between Mary and James and holding them to me, and with Hemi and Tangi all but carrying the little broken bird. It was a heavy and painful walk up the hill with the hundreds of people following, their hundreds of voices singing the final songs. There was pain in seeing the little children and their quietness, pushing ahead of us the wheelchair, hung with wreaths and loaded with flowers and greenery. And it was difficult indeed, and painful, to watch our child being lowered, and to hear the first fall of earth, and the wailing which came from around and from within me. There was pain, finally, in turning away.

After our return to the house, and after the freeing of the house for the living, there was hot food ready in the wharekai, and the wharekai was bright with flowers. There was talking and laughter and singing to turn us all to the living. It was not easy to turn to the living but there was obligation to do so.

It was not easy to turn to the living although grief had been shared amongst many, amongst hundreds. Not easy even though there was exhaustion, and acceptance of death. Because although our child's death had been with us a long time and was not a new thing in our minds, although a gift, once given, is with you for always, and although it is true that there is much that is right in death, it was the manner of the death that gave, gives pain. More than that, it is the brokenness, the sorrowing of the little bird that is most awful for us to bear.

I woke that night hearing the wheels bump over the little step, move onto the verandah and down the ramp. I listened for the gate latch but did not hear it so I knew that the gate had already been opened. I knew that Toko was going out to find his brother, his companion, the little Manu. I would have got up quickly then to help Toko with his chair. We did not want him to be using his small strength, wheeling his chair on his own. We wanted to be his strength, and to be with him at any waking time. His death had been with us for a long time by then.

But Mary was ahead of me. I heard her singing and I heard her bedroom door open, and she went along the passage and out. So I did not hurry. I got up and put on a jacket and some shoes, and by the time I reached the gate I could see Mary ambling, in her own way, to the front entrance of the wharenui. It was a bright, starry night and I could see her quite clearly though there were no lights on in the house. The side entrance of the house I could not see, but I could hear Toko backing his chair up the ramp. I could hear, faintly, the sound of Manu's voice calling and talking, but this was nothing new to us. Toko would talk to him and they would come home together. Manu would get quietly back into bed and sleep heavily until morning. Or I could have gone there and helped Toko onto the mattress beside his brother. I could have covered them both and they would have been comfortable sleeping there.

But it was when Toko pushed the swinging door open that there was a different sound, like a soft explosion, then Manu screamed out and there was a glimpse of light although the house itself was in darkness still. There were running footsteps but I could see no one by the light of stars. No one passed my way.

I began to run then, shouting for Hemi, running and stumbling over the starry ground to the verandah. It was habit kicking off the shoes. I have no memory of taking off my shoes, even though every other movement, every sound and feeling, and everything seen that night is in my memory forever. But I have nothing in my memory about the shoes. I only know that our little niece came to me the next day bringing them. She was crying. 'Aunty your shoes,' she'd said.

In the house I saw the tipped wheelchair and Toko sprawled across Mary's lap. Manu was up hovering, dancing, talking, crying.

And all of this I saw by the light of fire which fingered the special door frame and had begun to spread across the wall. Our child's face had death on it, and I saw this, saw every death feature by the wild light of flame burning through his hair.

His death had been with us for a long time, but it is the manner of his death that is so hard to bear. And it is the little bird that is the broken one now. With some difficulty we who are strong turn slowly to the living, but for the little Manu there has been no mending, no turning. That is the most difficult thing of all.

26

Roimata

The men from the hills, mostly of our race but some not, stayed with us over the three days of mourning. They worked for us without resting, getting wood for the fires and helping with the preparations and the cooking of food. They set up extra cooking facilities for us. They made extra tables and forms, and built onto the wash-room because we had never accommodated such numbers of people as arrived all through the days from early in the morning.

The men were still there on the third night after the tables had been cleared and the cleaning up finished. They stayed talking, singing, drinking – helping us to be again part of the living. Drinking yet not drinking, that was something I noticed. They stayed, they laughed and talked. But they did not drink, or drank little, only pretending to drink. When we went to bed they were there still, laughing, talking, singing, but not drinking at all.

When I asked Tangimoana and Pena and James if they were coming home to sleep they said they would stay a while. Tangi was quiet and happy in her manner with the anger seemingly gone from her. James said, 'We're all right Ma, don't worry about us,' so I thought that I would not worry. There was something happening but I thought I would not worry because there had been enough pain. There was obligation to put trouble away, to talk, to sing, to notice the flowers that people had put about, to notice that your home had been tidied, your washing done, your beds made ready for you. We were exhausted and glad of exhaustion. We took our little sad bird home with us to sleep.

It was in sleep that dawn exploded, and at dawn that sleep exploded. The house shook and somewhere there was a fall of glass. Hemi got up and rushed out but I was reluctant to rise. Something was happening but I thought that I should not be concerned, there had been enough pain already. Manu was sleeping quietly on the stretcher that we had put in our room for him. I could hear footsteps on the paths but they were hesitant. There were no voices, no shouting.

Then the engines started up, the engines of the big machines that had been quiet in the hills and left standing for the past three days. I dressed slowly and went out, not because of fear or worry, but out of curiosity, or a need to be with others, a need not to be alone.

It was a shrouded dawn of weightless, downy rain, with barely enough light to give substance to the land and sea.

Up on the hills the new road had been blasted and the machines were moving in, pushing asphalt and rock down the hillsides, heaping it and pushing it forward, tipping and tumbling it into scaffolding and foundations of new buildings, some of which were burning and falling.

All this was sensed in the half-darkness rather than clearly seen, while further back in the hills another blast was heard. Somehow there was joy in it.

Then someone said that it would soon be light, light enough to see who they were who were working the machines, walking about with torches in the half-dark. We should all get back into our beds before the light came, and we should not come out of our houses, or look out until everything was quiet.

So we all went back to our beds and listened to the machines and to the cracking and falling of timber, and to a string of detonations, some near and some far away. The machines seemed to come nearer, and it was almost full light. Then the engines stopped. There were voices, quiet voices, and people running. It was the way of running that is not meant to be heard. After that there was no sound.

There was no sound, so we rose from our beds and looked out. The new road had been destroyed, the new structures had been flattened. The big machines were submerged in the sea. We saw all this from our windows but we did not, at first, go out.

Later we went to the wharenui, looked in and saw the men

166

and the young ones asleep in there. So we went in and collected all the clothing they had been wearing and distributed it to be washed. Hemi and some of the others hosed down the verandah floor, and cleaned the footwear that had been left there.

We washed the clothing and hung it on our lines. Then we collected clean clothing and took it the wharenui leaving some by each bed. Breakfast was cooking in the wharekai and the tables had been set.

We were a noisy lot that morning, joking with each other, laughing, chatting about everything – everything but not the one thing. When breakfast was almost ready we all went out to the wharenui and did a boisterous haka to wake the people up. It was a haka to wake them but it was also an expression of love and a shout of joy. We pulled the blankets from the sleepers and threw the clothes at them, shouting at them and not caring that there were two visitors at the door looking in on our private lives.

'Get up, drunks.'

'Come on, sore-heads, get up.'

'Get over to that wharekai or your breakfast goes out to the seagulls.'

'You lot, you'd sleep through Cyclone Harata. . . .'

'Or Tornado Tamati. You don't know what goes on do you?'

'While you sleep.'

We sang to them, love songs, which on that morning were songs of joy. We played tricks with the water in the showers, giving a cold blast here and a hot blast there by turning the outside taps off and on. Soon they were sitting at the tables showered and grinning, and wearing a strange mixture of clothes.

'We're just starting breakfast,' Hemi said to the two officers. 'Join us.' There were other people there by then. A crowd had gathered on the beach and were looking back up to what had been the road, or out to where they could see the tips of the machines showing above the surface of the sea. There were photographers there, and people writing in notebooks, as well as officials who had cordoned off a large area. They wouldn't join us, they'd have a look round.

'Go ahead,' Hemi said, leaving them standing on the steps.

After breakfast we began the clean-up. We washed and stacked away all the dishes, cleaned the big cooking pots, carried the tables out to be scrubbed, and swept and mopped all the floors. We hosed down the wash and toilet facilities. Mattresses were carried out to be aired and all the linen gathered in a pile and taken away for washing. There was rubbish to bury or burn and empty bottles to be taken away. The wharenui was vacuumed and dusted and Mary took out her polishing cloths.

'Are we speaking to the chief?' one of them said to Stan.

'We're all chiefs here,' he said.

'Can we speak to the person in charge?'

'We're all in charge.'

'Is there somewhere where we can talk?' they asked.

'Right here will do,' said Stan.

At that stage the mattresses were being brought in to be stacked at one end of the wharenui, but instead of stacking them we put them in place round the room and sat down to listen.

'We're making inquiries about incidents occurring on the land adjacent to here.'

'Ask away,' Stan said.

'All right then, tell us what you know.'

'The road has been broken up, the buildings are flat on the ground, the machines are in the sea.'

'But you know more than that, obviously.'

'That's right. We woke early this morning because of what sounded like an explosion in the hills. It sounded close. We all got up and went out. It was still too dark to see but we heard the machines start up. We could hear them pushing rubble down the hill, pushing down what had been built. We saw the torches and the fires. Then we all went back to bed.'

'All of you?'

'All.'

'Didn't you want to know what was happening?'

'We did, so we got up and went out. Once we found out

168

what it was we went back to bed.'

'Could you identify. . . .'

'We could not. It was not light enough to see.'

'Surely you would have been interested in knowing who. . . ?'

'We were not interested.'

'Why not?'

'If we'd been able to identify people we'd have been able to help you with your inquiry. We've helped you before on two occasions, as you know. We were not satisfied, not happy with what you made the inquiries show. . . .'

'The inquiries were thorough. . . .'

'We were not believed. There was evidence, we gave help, but we were not . . . understood, and not believed. What we told you then was turned against us, was given other meaning.'

'We'll have another look round.'

'Be our guests,' said Stan. 'Look anywhere you like, talk to anyone. But if you need to come into this house again please remove your shoes. We've just finished cleaning up following the tangi of our child who was killed here Tuesday night.'

'Well. . . .'

'Whose death was caused.'

'Well . . . that's proceeding, isn't it? Time will. . . .'

'Time will probably not. . . .'

'We won't stay long but we'll need to speak. . . . Who are all these people?'

'People who live here, relatives and friends who have been at the tangi of our child, whose death was caused. . . .'

The two officers did not stay long after that. Over the next few days the machines were winched from the sea and taken away. The hills have been quiet since.

The hills will be scarred for some time, and the beach front spoiled. But the scars will heal as growth returns, because the forest is there always, coiled in the body of the land. And the shores, the meeting places of the land and sea, if left will become clean again. We will put the boats out into clear water again and go for kahawai, moki and shark, and will put lines down for kelpie and cod. There will be good shellfishing again. There will be tuna to hang above the smoke fires.

169

27

James

The young man said to the people, 'There's a story that says that the finishing of this poupou – this last for the old house, first for the new – goes into the future. That the completion will be done once it is known who the lower figure should be. I know now who must go there. I know now who it is that has been fathered by one who, in his own time, had no children of his own. I can do it now. But you might want me to wait until I'm older. You could think that this should be done by an older man.'

'We want you to complete it now,' they said, 'But anyway you do not need our permission. The permission came to you before you were born. In the story it is said that one day someone would know who it is that should fill that place, know who it is that is the man's tamaiti. If you know it, then you are the one. We will say the karakia and follow the correct rules before you begin.'

'There's a rule that I've heard of,' the young man said, 'that says not to show in wood those from living memory. But it has been done before, and now it. will be done again.'

'If you know it is right then it is right,' they said. 'We will have the karakia.'

When the blessings had been done the young man put mattresses down in the meeting-house for himself, his brother and his aunt, and took up his tools. He placed his chisel between the new thighs of the tipuna and below the feet of the man-penis, and began shaping the head of the tamaiti.

On one side of the head the chisel made a fine and perfect curve to the chin, but on the other side the head became widened and the jaw was hooked and lengthened. 'A baby for the loving-man,' the woman said. 'Make him lovely and nice. A baby for me.'

The brother of the young man began to cry but the young man said, 'When this is finished you won't cry any more, and soon there'll be work for you to do, and you can help right now . . . to keep the chisels sharp, to collect the shavings, burn them the way we've been told. When it's finished, then you won't cry any more.'

'Is it real?' he said. 'Is it real?'

'It's real, but nothing can be like it was before.'

'Lovely and nice,' the loving-woman said.

The young man shaped out the shoulders, the one curving smoothly out and down from the neck, the other humping sharply from behind the ear. He outlined a full, broad chest, tapering to small thighs. He outlined the tops of the small legs lightly but only as far as the knees.

When the outline was complete he put a mallet in his brother's hand and showed him what to do.

In the evenings, after a meal in the wharekai, the three would return to the house, clear away the shavings, tend to their tools, and go to sleep. And while they slept the house was quiet all through the night.

One afternoon the young man put his tools down and went with his brother and his aunt and said to the rest of the people, 'We are ready for the dedication.'

And one morning soon after that the people assembled for the blessing. But it was not only the people whose house it was who were there. People came in large numbers bringing their gifts and their love.

They looked at the completed carving and saw the tamaiti, the mokopuna, the potiki, with all his stories entwined about him, and they knew that the house was complete. They saw that the head of the tamaiti, alive with fire, had been widened and drawn down on one side. On that side of it was a small, shelled ear that listened to the soft whisperings, the lullabies, the quiet lamentations, while on the other side the ear was large and cupped to hear and know the wisdom of the world.

171

The given pendant hung from the lobe. They saw that one eye had been set low towards the earth-mother and that it matched the green colour of the earth. And the other eye, they saw, had been set high, towards the sky-father, and it contained the blue and blood colours of the sky.

They saw, and smiled, at the wide mouth that had at its corners the magic swirls, and that had the talking, storytelling tongue whirling out and down to where the heart began.

They saw that one shoulder curved easily and without pain from the neck to the upper arm, while the other humped from behind the ear forming the twisted burden that weighted and broadened the upper arm. On this shoulder sat the companion, the little bird.

The chest they saw was full of life and breath, and the large heart was patterned over the chest in a spiral that covered it completely. It was a spiral heart that had no breaking – no breaking and no end.

The fish that was clutched to the belly by one three-fingered hand arched and looped above the hand, and rested its head on one shoulder, the shoulder that gave no pain. The eye of the fish was small and pink and told of its life and its death, while its mouth showed the hook shape. The long fish-tail coiled itself about a patterned rock. In the other hand was a woven basket that was heavy and full, but which as a gift was carried easily.

Below the heart the pito became a plaited cord, and the plaited cord became a penis-child sleeping between the narrowed thighs. At each side there were the spinning, patterned wheels of the chair.

Each small leg was hobbled with knotted seaweed strands and the feet were licked with fire.

When most of the visitors had gone, the people whose house it was settled on the mattresses to tell, retell, listen to the stories. The stories were of people and whanaungatanga, of the plaiting that gives strength to the basket, the weaving that gives the basket beauty, and of koha that makes the basket full.

172

And the stories were also of the land and sea, sky and fire, life and death, love and anger and pain.

28

The stories

A woman told of the gulls and of how they feed from sea and shore, rest on land but find freedom, the struggle that is freedom, in the skies. She told of how she had come there, being flown on the backs of gulls. The gulls had carried her, returning her there after a long time away. She told of gifts that she'd been given, and how gifts once given cannot be taken away and do not change. Gifts did not change even though there could be a shifting in the self caused by pain.

'Light is a gift too,' she said, 'A gift of the sky, which is something that the earth knows. But the dark, the dark is a gift also because in the dark there is nurturing. These things are known to the earth as well as to the sky.

'And the watchers know it, waiting, and believing that what is not seen will one day be seen. The waiters know that the earth will give its gifts, and that the sky will too.

'I am an ever-watcher of the sky,' she said, 'a patient above-all watcher. I do not turn my back. Do not allow the eyes to move or close, but lock them always open on the pressing wall of sky.

'It would have been an easy thing to turn shoulders against the stacking thunder, or to let the sleet-heavy eyelids droop and close. Could have been so easy, and so loving, to have gone towards the dark and been cradled there.

'In a time of solid dark,' she said, 'I went down to the shore. Our eyes, the eyes of the whanau, are sea-eyes, being pitched constantly, inevitably, unceasingly towards the sea, rolling in reverse action to the tides. Our eyes are shore eyes, the shoreline being patterned, mapped, indelibly on the eyes.

'One evening I collected ngakihi from a rock and baited my hooks with them. I uncoiled a length of line and threw it out over the sea of polished dark. It was a waiting, watching dark, a watcher's, waiter's dark, an open-armed dark. It would have been so easy to have closed the eyes and to have been enfolded there.

'But the shore is a nothing place, a neutrality too salt for growth, a watcher's place. So this watcher waited there, not knowing at first that the sliver, the speck, dotted on the eye and traversing the sky, would come, not from the sky itself but from the depths.

'Because suddenly the kahawai leapt from a flat and waiting sea, arcing momentarily against the wall of sky.

'There is a greenstone silverness about the kahawai. It is life. And its eye is little and bright like the paua-shell eyes ever-wakeful at the edges of the night. It was the awaited glimmer, that rose and fell in bloodshot drops, and then became written, stained upon the eye.

'Blood is life, and you have a life of blood. In hefty knots it thrusts out between the thighs, and the child borne on it sneezes to live, or lives, screaming the night in two. Tomorrow two children of mine will go before the courts. I will accompany them proudly and gladly. Birth is only the beginning of pain, to which there is no end.

'And there's no end to love. But the sinews binding love can sometimes be severed, staining earth with blood-ochre colour, and the face of love can be turned another way. My husband, as rooted to the land as a tree is, turns in his pain to the soil, while I wait for, and eventually hold, the sliver in my eye. But love has not lessened and never will. In being turned another way we have turned to each other, the one looking to the sky, the other to earth – the mother to the father, the father to the mother. We will accompany our children proudly when tomorrow comes.

'The kahawai leaps gilded, silvered and green from a dark and hidden place, while the watchers tread so carefully at the edge, disturbing no stone, no footprint of theirs making shadows on the sand.'

A man told of an end that was a beginning. The time of no work was a time when his real work had begun, or was taken up again as he had always intended. His story was of the ground, the earth, and of how earth was a strength, how earth strengthened them all. 'Care for it and it cares for you,' he said, 'Give to it and it gives. Through it you shoulder your pain.

'People are strength too. Care for people and you are cared for, give strength to people and you are strong. It's land and people that are a person's self, and to give to the land and to give to the people is the best taonga of all. Giving is strength. We've always known it.

'The hills are quiet now. They went from our hands long ago but we do not need them in our hands. We only need them to be there, to be left to heal, to be left for trees to grow on. With trees on the hills again our own corner is safe and we are who we are. For now it is safe. With trees on the hills we can keep our ground productive, our sacred places safe, our water clear. For all of us. Us, who live here now, and also those who belong here and will return one day, whether during their life or when they die.

'But it's not only for us now. We have a trust. We look after this place for those who have not yet been born. It's for the life and health of people and we have it in trust from those who've gone on ahead of us.

'I don't want to talk too much about this other thing but only say I'm proud of the young ones, and of others that don't live here, for what they did. I won't talk too much even though there's only us here. We'll all be there to support them tomorrow. It's all of us up there. They are all of us. We are all of us. And what I think is . . . what those representing them think is . . . there's not enough known . . . our young ones, and the others . . . they'll come to no harm.

'Also I have to tell you, I didn't think that I would ever support . . . any action. But good has come of it, and I think it was . . . right. If it wasn't, time will show. Time will show if it was meant.

'And time. I spend a lot of time looking at the soil but don't think I'm turning my back. It's a way of making the pain less. Everyone's got hurt, which is always present there on the circle. But there are ways, on the circle, if we can find

176

them, of making it less, of living through. No reira, tena koutou katoa.'

The young man did not tell his story in words but gave it to the people as it was, chiselled into shape at the base of the tree.

It was an old story, an ancient story, only now there was a new phase to it, an old story beginning with the seed that is a tree.

But that was not the real beginning. The story came, like all stories, from before the time of remembering which is in the time when there was only darkness. Only the giving, loving dark. There was nothing seen or heard there, and there was no movement. There was no living but only the potential – which became the conception.

It was a story that opened and put its seed into the time of remembering. It became a people story through wood, both people and wood being parented by earth and sky so that the tree and the people are one, people being whanau to the tree.

Yet in the time of remembering, the story was only partly told, could only be partly told.

In the new phase the child was recognised by his mother, and shown to his father – and through the young man who told by hands, he was returned, with all his life stories, to the whanau.

The young woman had her stories written in a book. She stood and said, 'Here is a song to hang on the tree. It's about the colour red:

> 'The girl ran the sharp track home
> Feet lacerated by stone and the voice
> Close to her ear
> Whispering
> "Unwind me from the kelp strands
> Pull the barnacles from my thighs
> Take the stone from my throat
> Remove the scales from my eyes."

Ran sharp over the stone track home
Tumble heart to tumble heart
Hearing
"Red is the sea
From the time of my borning
But blood-ochre is the sacred colour,
Your hands are cupped
Round the heart of my crying
Paint your houses
With the sacred colour."

And once she woke
On a crimson night of
Flaring sky
To the tekoteko
Painted in fire and
Calling
"Kua hinga
Kua hinga
Night has
Taken the eyes
Takoto, takoto."

Then on another night while far away
The wombed house
Became a wailing cavern
One entrance the fire-toothed aperture
Through which all must pass,
And she heard
"Wrap me again
In bright weed
Which will be a blanket for me
Salt my eyes and my tongue
Mo te ao pouri."

And she cried
"Take up the shells
Cut open the foreheads
And let the faces be flamed
Let them be

Painted in sorrow
Painted with
The sacred colour."

The girl sang the sharp track home
In detonating dawn
Singing
"Listen as the wind sings
And white birds carve the sky
The song before dawn
Is the soft song of rain,
Anger is the sacred
Colour
Salted close to the heart,
Anger is ochre-coloured,
Let some of it remain
On the tree."'

The boy had a story of night.

'It's real,' he said. 'There was a barracouta silver on the horizon and centred with a greenstone eye. She was two-headed, having no tail, but having instead another snapping jaw where her tail would have been. It's real.

'A little taniwha came by that way. He was so small and so loving and so magical. Swimming. Far out there close to the horizon. It's a story of night and the stars were all out. Shining.

'And we all went with him, all the little birds. Not the gulls which call and cry, but all the little birds which sing of insects and berries and flowers. Happy and scared. Singing and scared, with wingbeat sounds coming from our such small and frightened hearts.

'Nothing can be like before.

'Swimming close to her, the little taniwha. The greenstone eye was closed, but the jaws at either end lay open as she slept.

'Little one, swimming close. Then in. It's real, it's real. In he swam. Then the green eye opened and the jaws closed down.

'Nothing can be like before, but I search for the barracouta.

179

Sometimes I find her, but nothing can be changed. And I find that she has been given wrong paint by starlight. She waits silver only in starlight, but otherwise she is many-coloured. Starlight has given wrong light to the stone eye, because her eye otherwise holds tenderness. And in other light the jaws are not jawlike. In other light they extend, armlike, to embrace. No need to fear. And it's real.

'Nothing is like before but everything's real. The little bird sits in his tree.'

The old woman sang of a time gone ahead, and of those already walking ahead of her on the pathways. Her eyes were reddened as though they bled.

And her songs, like the pathways, were interweavings of times and places and of all that breathed between earth and sky. And the pathways and the songs went into a time beyond the thumbing down of the eyelids.

The child-woman had a story to tell but she did not tell it. She too sang along pathways not known. Yet her story could be heard if you listened to the whisperings of the house.

And the stories continued well into the night, moving from one person to the next about the house until the circle had been fully turned. Then the people slept.

But the telling was not complete. As the people slept there was one more story to be told, a story not of a beginning or an end, but marking only a position on the spiral.

Potiki

There is one more story to tell which I tell while the house sleeps. And yet the house does not sleep as the eyes of green and indigo brighten the edges of the world. There is one more story to ,tell but it is a retelling. I tell it to the people and the house. I tell it from the wall, from where yesterday and tomorrow are as now.

I know the story of my death. I tell it from the tree.

The night was a night of stars, like the long-ago fish night, but the fish night too is now. Though I did not remember the glitter of the night of the fish but was later told, yet I see it in the now of now. And I do see now the dancing, bangling water, the orange light, the brine, the vine. I know the pull of the great barking fish of that first star night.

On this other night of stars there was a soft quiet with only a small tapping of water that had to be listened carefully for. The hills were shadowed, not catching the light of stars. The big machines that would slice the morning's light were hidden somewhere in the hills' shadows.

My brother Manu was not in his bed when I woke. Perhaps it was his getting up that woke me. His bed was empty and our door was open. I listened but did not hear him in the house, or on the path, or on the road outside. I did not hear him cry or call out.

I worked myself out of the bed and into my chair and pulled my rug over me. My mother Mary was awake, I could hear her slow movements in the next room. I hear them now. I did not call her and I did not wait.

There was a warmth and stillness in the night and it was sweet and salt-smelling. It was a night of stars.

My brother would come to no harm but I would go and find him. If he woke when I found him, and if he knew what was real, we would sit together for a while and star-talk. There was not much time left for us to talk. Not much time for me.

If he did not wake or did not know what was real I would take his hand and wheel along beside him. He would come home with me, get into his bed and sleep quietly for the rest of the night.

It was not easy for me by then to wheel my chair, but I could do it slowly. I was supposed to call someone if I wanted to go in my chair, but that night I went on my own, moving slowly.

I wheeled out through the open door of the bedroom, out of the open front door, and down the ramp that had been made especially for my chair. Then I moved along the path, which because of my chair had been widened.

It was a good night to be out, wheeling slowly. My brother would come to no harm. I listened for him but the night was still. There was only a soft water sound which could be heard if listened very carefully for.

I knew that my brother would be in the meeting-house. He would be sleeping in there, or could have been sitting, dark-eyed, covering his ears with his hands, waiting for me to come.

I moved slowly towards the door that had been built especially for me. Then, as I moved slowly up the path I saw the door quickly open, and someone, perhaps my brother, come out. But it was not my brother walking so quickly towards the hills which were shadowed and without the light of stars. 'Where's Manu?' I called, but it was not one of my uncles or cousins running quickly and darkly into the night with scarcely a sound.

I wheeled slowly along the pathway that had been made for the width of my chair. I remembered to move slowly so that there would not be strain on the heart growing too big for me.

At the bottom of the ramp I turned my chair carefully so that I could back up the ramp, because this was easier for me when alone. I was thinking about the shadow that had moved so quickly into the shadowed hills.

I listened, and now there was sound. But it was sound that was not different, sound that I was accustomed to. I heard my birth mother Mary coming slowly in starlight, walking in her special rocking way. I heard the quiet sound of her singing as she made her way to the main door of the house.

Behind me as I backed my chair slowly up the ramp I heard my brother begin to talk and cry, but this was not a different sound. I would go in and talk to him. He would come home with Mary and me, and get back into his bed. He would sleep there quietly until morning.

As I inched my chair close to the doorway he began to call more loudly.

'There's fire,' he called, but the words were not different words. 'There's fire, there's fire. And it's real.'

Then there was a bursting sound, and a scream, which were sounds that were different.

I hurried then, backing my chair through the doorway.

But the doorway, suddenly, had become the toothed aperture. It was suddenly the toothed aperture through which all must pass.

The night was edged now, and clamorous.

All the stars were falling.

And from this place of now, behind, and in, and beyond the tree, from where I have eversight, I watch the people.

The people work and watch and wait. They pace the tides and turn the earth. They stand, listening on the shores.

They listen, hearing mostly the quiet. It is the quiet that is trees growing, the sidling of fish through water, the hovering cloud, the open-eyed quiet of the night.

Because the shores are the silent places that take no seed, that long ago were left devoid when anger and fear sent some of life to the protecting belly of the sea, and some of life to the protecting arms of land.

The man letting crumbled earth sift between his fingers hears mainly that, but he listens too for the shadows closing

183

in, the whisperings about the edges of the land.

The woman throwing her line hears the flutter and splash of it as she casts.

Those who fish with nets hear the creak of oars and the sliding of the net being let out over the stern.

The ones who work in words or wood listen for the beat that words and wood have.

Because, although they listen too for the approaching shadows and the whisperings about the edges of the land, they cannot, from where they are, hear the sounds distinctly. They cannot, as I can in this time of now, distinctly hear the sounds of this now place, which is a place beyond the gentle thumbing of the eyes.

From where they are the people see the boles and branches drift ashore. They see these whiten to the beat of tides and sun. They hear the stones roll and shuttle, and see them patterning the shore.

But they do not clearly see the big logs being rolled into position, or see themselves crouching down behind. They do not quite see the stones nesting in their own cupped palms. They do not see distinctly the white sticks stand, and do not see themselves fingering the white sticks, taking the white sticks in their hands.

They do not hear distinctly the stirring within the house, the murmuring, the assembling.

They do not clearly hear the footfalls, some of them their own. They cannot see the shadowless forms, forms of which they themselves may be the shadows, taking up and shouldering the sun-bleached wood.

And they do not distinctly see the tekoteko as they come, taking up the bones, moving in silently beside them.

> Ko wai ma nga tekoteko
> Ka haere mai?
> Ko nga tipuna
> O te iwi e.
>
> Ko wai ma nga tangata
> Ka whakarongo atu?

Ko te iwi
O tenei whenua.

Ko wai te tamaiti
Ka noho ai i tera?
Ko ia
Te potiki e,

Ko ia
Te potiki e.

No reira, e kui ma, e koro ma, e hoa ma. Tamariki ma,
mokopuna ma – Tena koutou. Tena koutou, tena koutou
katoa.

Ka huri.

The Women's Press is a feminist publishing house. We aim to publish a wide range of lively, provocative books by women, chiefly in the areas of fiction, literary and art history, physical and mental health and politics.

To receive our complete list of titles, send a large stamped addressed envelope. We can supply books direct to readers. Orders must be pre-paid in £ sterling with 60p added per title for postage and packing (70p overseas). We do, however, prefer you to support our efforts to have our books available in all bookshops.

The Women's Press, 34 Great Sutton Street, London EC1V 0DX

Faces in the Water

'I will write about the season of peril … a great gap opened in the ice floe between myself and the other people whom I watched, with their world, drifting away through a violet-coloured sea where hammer-head sharks in tropical ease swam side by side with the seals and the polar bears. I was alone on the ice … I traded my safety for the glass beads of fantasy'

Faces in the Water is about confinement in mental institutions, about the fear the sensible and sane of this world have of the so-called mad, the uncontrolled. Banished to an institution, Istani Mavet lives a life dominated by the vagaries of her keepers as much as by her own inner world.

Janet Frame's clear and unforgettable prose startles and evokes. A remarkable piece of writing by New Zealand's finest living novelist.

'Lyrical, touching and deeply entertaining' John Mortimer, *Observer*

Fiction   £4.95
ISBN: 0 7043 3861 0

Living in the Maniototo

Winner of the Fiction Prize, New Zealand Book Awards, 1980

Janet Frame again offers us a richly imagined exploration of
uncharted lands. The path is through the Maniototo, that 'bloody
plain' of the imagination which crouches beneath the colour and
movement of the living world. The theme of the novel is the
process of writing fiction, the power, interruptions and avoidances
that the writer feels as she grapples with a deceptive and elusive
reality. We move with our guide, a woman of manifold
personalities, through a physical journey which is revealed to be a
metaphor for the creative process – on which our own survival
depends.

'Puts everything else that has come my way this year right in the
shade' *Guardian*

Fiction   £3.95
ISBN: 0 7043 3867 X